MW01517070

A Peculiar *Case*

From the Files of Elizabeth Grant

Ginette Guy Mayer

Ginette Guy Mayer

Copyright©Ginette Guy Mayer 2023
First Edition 2023

This book is a work of fiction. References to real people, events, establishments, organizations, or locales are intended only to provide a sense of authenticity and are used fictitiously. All other characters, incidents, and dialogue are drawn from the author's imagination and are not to be constructed as real.

No parts of this publication may be reproduced in any form or by any means, electronic or mechanical, including photocopying, recording, or any information browsing, storage, or retrieval system, without permission in writing from the author.

www.ginetteguymayer.com

Cover design by Ginette Guy Mayer
(using PosterMyWall)

ISBN 978-1-7388714-2-1 (Paperback)
ISBN 978-1-7388714-3-8 (eBook)

Table of Contents

Acknowledgement

A big thank you to Paul R. King for keeping a keen eye on the commas and the dots. And, for his encouragement with this project.

Thank you to all the characters in this book who think nothing of waking me up at 4 am because they have something clever to say.

Prologue

The two men who walked into the east side tavern looked as out of place as champagne flutes on the bar. They chose an empty table along the wall, and the younger man signalled the waiter for a couple of beers. Suits and ties were seldom seen here unless everyone returned from a funeral or a wedding. The late-day crowd was mostly local factory workers coming in for a quick drink after a long day.

The older, heavy-set man wiped his brow with his handkerchief and looked around the room, what he could see anyway, under the blue haze of cigarette smoke. This was a place where you drank out of the bottle. Any glass offered would still show fingerprints from past customers and might stick to the table.

"You are such an idiot!" said Lawson, the younger of the two men.

"I can't believe it!"

"What did you want me to do?" asked Drew.

"Walk into the rare bookseller and ask for an appraisal? Of a book I don't own. No, I gave it to an old lady from the historical society so she could get a valuation on it.

"If I want to sell it, I need to know how much it could be worth," added Drew.

"I don't want to be swindled."

"Well, of course not; instead, you prefer to be hoodwinked by an old lady," said Lawson with heavy sarcasm.

"And, by the way, you completely lost track of her and your book along with it."

"I'm planning to fix it or try anyway," said Drew.

"Discretion is key. As you know, when that British tourist died from a heart attack, I took his box and the book. As a customs officer, I am cooked if caught."

"Well, I'm a lawyer, and I'm helping you, so not that great for me either!" added Lawson.

"So, what's next?"

"I'm going to see a private investigator who might track them down. It's been so long now, it will look like she's stealing the book," concluded Drew.

Chapter 1

The sign on the door read *François Lefebvre Private Investigator*, but if you came in to see Frank, he was rarely in, if ever. The secretary would tell you that Frank was on a case, out of town on a fact-finding mission, or just plain too busy to see you. Elizabeth Grant had been the agency's office manager since it opened in 1930 and ran everything from the start. She would take your information and jot down notes about your case, covering all angles with pointed questions. She would assure you that every detail would be passed along, and she would contact you as needed. Elizabeth would always be the one in touch because if the truth must be told, there was no François Lefebvre Private Investigator.

The road to 137 Pitt Street in Cornwall, Ontario, and the P.I. office had been convoluted for Elizabeth. Ottawa was her hometown, and she met her husband when she worked in the typing pool for the Department of Justice. William Grant was originally from Cornwall, and his legal education landed him a promising career in the same department. They dated for a while and followed the logical path of marriage and a family. Elizabeth had been reluctant to consider marriage, not because she didn`t care for William, but because it would mean the end of her career. She had loved the work and hoped for her own promotions but once married, it was expected that women stayed home to look after their family. They had two daughters, grown now and granddaughters.

Elizabeth`s husband died in a motor vehicle accident on a country road. So, she found herself widowed at 47 years old. That event changed her life, the way she saw the future, and other possibilities. William had a promising career, so financially, she had few worries, but her mind had always been eager for challenges. Her daughters expected a settled life for their mother and a more present grandmother, but Elizabeth had other plans.

The Grant family had often visited Cornwall and William`s family. Then, a few years before his death, they had seized an investment opportunity and purchased a rental property on Pitt Street, the business centre of Cornwall. The building was red brick and held a hardware store on the ground floor, two offices on the second floor, and a small apartment at the back. When the apartment and one of the offices became vacant, Elizabeth threw caution to the wind and found herself in Cornwall against her daughter's better advice.

The rental income from one of the second-floor offices (a lawyer's office) and the hardware store looked after the day-to-day expenses, and she now had her own office. In a bold move, she ordered the sign *François Lefebvre Private Investigator* and hung it on the door. She knew well that no one would take a woman investigator seriously, and although times had changed since her early career, opportunities remained limited. Oh, the work was there, but men preferred women who did it all under the umbrella of church charities and volunteer organisations. Despite the odds, Elizabeth felt confident she could make the agency work. Her experience at the Department of Justice and years debating with her husband on legal matters provided valuable insight.

And she had pulled it off very nicely for the last three years. Cornwall was a lovely town along the St. Lawrence River, with parks, open spaces, tree lined Second Street, and beautiful homes and churches. The location of Elizabeth's office and the apartment was ideal, right in the centre of everything. It was a vibrant area, within walking distance to shopping and any business services she might need.

Elizabeth particularly enjoyed the Carnegie Library at the southwest corner of Sydney and Second Street. Built some thirty years ago, its architecture was unique. It had an arched entrance, a corner turret on the right side, and a rounded left corner. It was a small castle-like library with an impressive collection. So much so that over a thousand books were stored at the nearby Snetsinger Block, a three-storey office and retail building on the northwest corner of Pitt and First Streets.

The Capitol Theatre, around the corner on Second Street, showed all the latest moving pictures in a surrounding second to none. Although it could seat over a thousand people, you had to get in line early to get the best seats. Elizabeth would take her granddaughters to see a show when they came to visit, and they were intrigued by the Greek plaster scenes in bas-relief around the lobby. They always wanted to go up and sit in one of the boxes, holding on to the brass railing and waiting for the stage curtains to open. Of course, stopping at Woolworth's lunch counter was a must on those visits.

Cornwall was also a factory town, a busy waterfront with a shipping canal and dry docks. All manner of mills from flour to cotton and paper found an excellent water supply for production needs and transportation to market.

Overhead wires crisscrossed the downtown streets to move along the streetcars, and the Cornwall Street Railway and Power Company also moved freight cars along the streets. Then, using the same lines, it connected the industries along the waterfront to the Grand Truck Railway in the north, reminding everyone that this was a working town. The 1930s had been hard for everyone, but Cornwall managed to hold its own, mainly because of the mills, canal, and construction work on various factory expansions.

The town was an interesting mix based on religion and language. The Irish Catholics had come to build the canals and their church was St. Columban's on Fourth Street. Many French-Canadian from Quebec had come to work in the factories and settled close to work in the east end. They were well served by the catholic church *Nativité de la Bienheureuse Vierge Marie (Nativity of the*

Blessed Virgin Mary). The neighbourhood shops were lined along Montreal Road, to the east.

First settlers had been British and Scots, Loyalists or migrants, come to build a new life. They attended several of the churches around town, Anglican, United, Presbyterian, Baptist. Methodist and there was even a Jewish Synagogue. Elizabeth found it fascinating and loved the variety it offered.

The basis of Elizabeth's P.I. work came from the colliding reality of a growing town and an economic downturn that impacted the surrounding countryside. The factories provided employment, and the depression created many in need and looking for work. The exodus from the country to the town began a housing shortage, some profiteering, and fraud of the city relief funds, which were sometimes misdirected from those in need. The police and city administration were short-handed and often relied on private investigators to provide the background information to support their cases. *François Lefebvre, Private Investigator,* had an excellent reputation and submitted clear reports supported by sound groundwork, all with the most complete discretion.

Chapter 2

It was easy for Elizabeth to bypass anyone's desire to meet with Frank Lefebvre in person. For many cases, the less seen, the better, and the authorities were looking for confidentiality. It worked to Elizabeth's advantage that she was a mature woman, as most easily confided in her, and businessmen took no notice. They saw any inquiry as innocent curiosity, with an inclination to gossip. The work was steady, and Elizabeth was content. Nobody knew that Frank Lefebvre was a figment of her imagination, not even Peter Darvis, her nephew and casual assistant. Sometimes, a male investigator was needed, and Peter was more than happy to help.

Peter Darvis was nineteen years old and a bookkeeping student at Cornwall's Commercial College, just down the street from Elizabeth's office in the Snetsinger Block. Peter was tall and slim, and the spectacles already gave him the serious air of an accountant. The fact that he had recently lost his father and felt a duty to help his mother and two sisters did nothing to lighten his seriousness. At the time, he had wanted to quit school to help financially, but his mother would not hear of it, so he was glad for any extra work Elizabeth could send his way.

On this Tuesday morning, Elizabeth came into work early to finish a report due this week. Also, she had missed a day's work with yesterday's terrible events. As she typed the last page, she made a mental note to drop the old typewriter at C.W. Kyte's to see if he could fix the sticking "r". A sticking "z" or "q" she could live with a bit longer, but why did it always have to be the "r"?

The office door opened, and Peter walked in. He had a hand over his mouth and sat at the corner desk.

"I can't believe the smell and the heat. It just lingers on, unbelievable and so sad," said Peter.

"Yes, Monday, August 7, 1933, will surely go down in history for the devastation and pain that fire caused," added Elizabeth.

"Most of that west block between Second and Third Streets is gone!"

"Roger at school said firefighters from Montreal and Ottawa were called in. Hard to believe no one died in that fire," noted Peter.

"Perhaps it was a blessing that it happened in the afternoon and not at night," said Elizabeth.

"I can't imagine what it would have been like if all those families had been sleeping. That's about fifteen families, and seventy-five people lost their jobs. I was so scared that with the heavy wind, the fire would move down and across the street. We were lucky.

"Rumours are that it started in the back of Fursey's Garage, maybe boys smoking or playing with matches. It was dry, and the fire moved quickly to the arena. It started around 11:30 am and burnt for five hours.

"The wind was so strong that the embers carried the fire to the north side of Third Street and a couple of buildings on the east side of Pitt. It could have been much worse."

"Did you hear about Reverend Ostrom from the Baptist Church?" asked Peter.

"It was incredible; he saved a building in the path of fire. He climbed the roof, sat on top and sprayed it with a garden hose! A garden hose, can you imagine? Buildings were burning around him, lots of smoke and heat, and he did it!"

"That was very courageous," said Elizabeth. "So many people came together, and there is no time lost in cleaning and planning for rebuilding.

"Unfortunately, there were also reports of people stealing from burned-out buildings, and two motorcycles have gone missing from Sandy Clark's garage. Although most had no insurance, we've had calls about helping with claims and losses.

"Will you be available for extra work? I could use the help," she asked.

"Will you need time to see your girl, Susan?"

The mention of Susan brought a huge smile to Peter's face. They had been going out for months; she was in some of his classes at the college, and their relationship looked serious enough.

"No, I'll manage," smiled Peter.

"She takes the train from Moulinette, so I mostly see her at school. Besides, it can't get too serious until I get enough income to help mother and set up on my own."

"I really appreciate any time you can give me," said Elizabeth as she opened the calendar on her desk.

"I know Mr Lefebvre will be out of town on other cases for at least the next couple of weeks. So let me get everything sorted in order of priority, and I will let you know the details for each assignment.

"There are some cases I know we won't take on. Mr Flanigan for example, he was asking for help retrieving some bonds and securities that were stolen from his apartment but that would be nearly impossible to track down."

"His apartment was not completely burnt," said Peter.

"That's how he was able to find out about the theft, he left in a hurry and when he went back the drawers and cupboards had been ransacked," said Elizabeth.

"His things were all over the floor, soaked, and he found 200 shares of an oil stock but all the other securities were gone.

"But there were just too many people milling about to tell who was helping and who was stealing, unfortunately."

As Peter stood up and walked over to the door, he turned and said, "Our classes are cancelled for a few days because of the fire; some are needed to help with their families and relief efforts for those who lost their apartments. I'll drop by tomorrow morning. Thanks, Aunt Liz!"

Elizabeth couldn't imagine how the town would manage so much loss, although Cornwall was no stranger to devastating fires like the Rossmore Hotel and even an earthquake. It was daunting. First, she would need to contact her friend Mary and Peter's mother, who worked with church charities. They might need an extra pair of hands.

At the knock on the door, Elizabeth straightened up and mentally rehearsed the set phrase that would excuse the agency's namesake absence on this day. The scheming might catch up with her one day, but it wouldn't be this day.

"Come in, please have a seat," said Elizabeth as a middle-aged man made his way into the small office. Heavy set and wearing a jacket even though it was a hot August day, he wiped his brow with his handkerchief.

"I didn't realise the chaos the fire had left behind. I didn't realise…

"I wasn't sure you would be open. I'm here to ask for help on a peculiar case. Is Mr Lefebvre available?" said the man in a business-like fashion.

"Mr Lefebvre is away right now. We have been swamped with the fire up the street and various court matters," explained Elizabeth.

"I'm Mrs Grant, the office administrator, and I can take down all the relevant information and open a case for you if you wish."

"That's fine with me. The matter at hand is important to me, and some travel might be needed to get to the bottom of this. I would also like to discuss your fees," said the client.

"Excellent. Can you provide me with your contact information and all the particulars about the situation and anyone involved?" asked Elizabeth.

"We charge by the hour for work done on your case and provide details about any expenses for travel to be reimbursed. I have an agreement letter with details here."

"My name is A.G. Drew, Albert Gallatin Drew, and I am a customs agent in Morrisburg. I'm originally from Vermont, but I moved my business to South Dundas a few years back. I have since taken a job as a customs agent."

"If you could just fill in the information form with address and contact information, that would be helpful," added Elizabeth as she opened a file.

"Thank you for coming to us for help, and what is this peculiar case you mention?"

"Some time ago, I lent a book I believe to be valuable, to a woman, an author, and historian, known to be an antiquarian, so that she could find out more about it. To put a value on it. It has been months now, and although we have met on occasions, she never returned the book to me," explained Drew.

"Every time we met, she claimed she would return it, but she had excuses for not doing so.

"She said the book was at her home in Merrickville or Cornwall. Finally, she said she packed it by mistake and shipped it to her sister, a Mrs Hoss, in Philadelphia! Unbelievable!"

"Have you taken steps to retrieve the book yourself?" asked Elizabeth.

"What is the name of the lady and her domicile?"

"I tried everything, and I even contacted local investigators in Nebraska and Pennsylvania, where she has family, to try and find her. I printed flyers with search notices and got the investigators to distribute them. No results in finding that Josephine Smith," exclaimed Drew.

At the mention of the name Elizabeth pulled back and considered it again; for some reason, the name rang a bell. But, then again, there were dozens of Josephine Smiths around, and she couldn't make much of it for now.

"And what of the book? Can you tell me about it and what makes you think it's valuable," she asked.

"It's a prayer book, printed in Paris in 1548, and I think it could have belonged to Mary Queen of Scots.

"I originally thought it was in a form of old English, but Josephine showed it to a priest in Montreal, who said it was old Scots. She confirmed it had value, and just before I loaned it to her, someone offered me $25. I expected it was worth more, and I didn't want to sell it," explained Drew.

"This running around of hers has been going on for over a year now, and I'm thinking that anyone intent on returning someone else's property would be able to do it sooner than that. I suspect she sold it somewhere in the States."

"How did you come to own the book, Mr Drew?" asked Elizabeth.

"Luck, I guess," replied Drew.

"I bought a box of books at the local flea market, and there it was amongst all the others."

"How did you come to know Josephine Smith? Certainly, you must have felt it was safe to loan her the book?" asked Elizabeth.

"Well, she made a presentation at our historical society about a book she just wrote. *The Transplanted Highlanders* is the title, I think, and she also writes about the Loyalists in the area.

"We were introduced, and she said she was an antiquarian in Ottawa. It seemed appropriate to mention my book and the search I was doing to prove its origin, and she showed great interest. So, I invited her to look at it and provide an opinion," explained Mr Drew.

"Since no qualified assessment could be done locally, it seemed logical to take the book with her to show it to people she knew.

"In the beginning, she kept in touch with me and shared the results of her inquiries. I saw her occasionally, but she never had the book with her. Very convenient is what I'm thinking now," he exclaimed.

"As I confronted her about its return, she started to weave a tale of intrigue and lost boxes, the likes of which I had never heard of."

"I see; I will share all this with Mr Lefebvre and get back to you," said Elizabeth.

"There must be a paper trail if shipping was involved, but I can see the complexity if we go back and forth between Eastern Ontario and the States.

"You can expect to hear from me in a few days; with this disaster, it's not business as usual, as you can imagine."

As Mr Drew made his way to the door, he turned and said, "I didn't expect that of her. She went from a scholar to a swindler, just like that."

Chapter 3

The morning went by so quickly that Elizabeth realised she was starving. She could pop in her apartment at the back but paused to consider her options. Although her daughters assumed she would be lonely on her own, she very much enjoyed the freedom of the single life.

The expectations of meat and potatoes on the table at the stroke of six were now behind her! Still, she wasn't a fan of eating out of a tin, so she went across the street to the Eaton Groceteria, "Where it pays to Shop", as the slogan would have it. They claimed to be a modern food centre, unhurried and unhampered by clerks. You made your choices and checked out. Sliced lunch ham was thirty-three cents a pound, and Mayfair tea at thirty-nine cents for half a pound sealed the deal. Luckily, before the fire, she had picked up a nice loaf of bread at H. Riley Bakery, now a smouldering ruin. William Riley and his wife lived over the bakery; they had lost everything.

While she waited for the homemade chicken soup to heat up, she considered the offer on the last case, Mr Drew, and the book. Was it worth investing time and effort? She didn't work on collecting fines for overdue books. Could something so rare and valuable find its way to Morrisburg? Then again, if someone like Al Capone could dig tunnels in Moose Jaw, Saskatchewan, for rum smuggling, why not a precious book in the Counties? First thing tomorrow morning, she would see what she could dig up on Josephine Smith, which should tell her if there was anything to go on.

For now, she would see if she could help those affected by the fire, and she placed a call to her friend Mary Randolph. Although much younger, Mary had become a good friend of hers. When she first came to town, Elizabeth figured it was a good idea to get involved and start making Cornwall a home. She met Mary via the Victorian Order of Nurses and the Federated Charities. Mary was old Cornwall stock from the early settlers from both sides of her family. She studied art in Montreal and returned to Cornwall when her father passed away in 1930. It seemed like Mary needed to get involved and keep busy. Elizabeth thought there was more to her leaving Montreal, but she didn't ask for now.

To Elizabeth's surprise, Mary picked up after a few rings. "Hi, it's Liz. Do you need any help? How are you managing with the fire damage and the families?"

"Hi, I was startled when the phone rang because the fire burnt some lines from the Bell Telephone exchange. I didn't know if ours worked," said Mary.

"Thanks for asking. I'm sure we could use you somewhere; we have seventeen homeless families. Most went with family members in the short term, but they will need everything."

"Since Mayor Horovitz consolidated all the Church charities into one, it's easier to coordinate. The Kinsmen Club is getting a fundraising campaign together, and we are organising furniture, clothing, and food donations.

"So, if you can spare the time, there's a meeting planned for later this afternoon," confirmed Mary.

"How did you fare at your end? Any damages?"

"No, I'm fine, but that block is so desolate now, soot everywhere. Some buildings closer to the fire had their windows crack from the heat, but I'm further down," said Elizabeth with relief.

"This is unrelated, but did you ever hear of a lady named Josephine Smith?" asked Elizabeth.

"She is an antiquarian and was writing pamphlets on the Loyalists. That's why I thought you might have heard of her."

"Didn't she author a book about the Scots settlers around Perth? If that's the one, then I did meet her once at a historical society event. We were introduced and chatted a bit. She self-published her book and seemed quite confident. Has she anything to do with a case of yours?" asked Mary.

"That is still to be determined, I would say. So, I will let you go. I'm sure you have things to do. What time and place for the meeting?"

"At the Cornwall Club, on the second floor, starts at 4 pm," confirmed Mary.

Before heading out to the meeting, Elizabeth left messages with St. Columban's and Nativity Catholic churches to inform them of the meeting and that she would follow up afterwards. The meeting was at "The Cornwall Club", at 42 Second Street East, a rare privilege for a woman to enter the facility, no doubt due to the urgency of the situation. The fraternal society dated from the late 1880s, and membership was restricted to 125 gentlemen.

When Elizabeth entered the building, the surroundings and décor were very masculine, and the smell reminded her of cigars and Scotch, which she did not find unpleasant. The Club was closed to members today, and the library, pool and card rooms were empty. Mary was already there, and so were the representatives from the Kinsmen Club, City Council, Board of Trade and the Presbyterian church. Mr Brooks from the Kinsmen Club would chair the meeting.

"Welcome, everyone," said Brooks as he motioned everyone to take a seat and start the proceedings.

"I would like to welcome Miss Randolph, secretary for the Federated Charities, Mrs Grant representing the Catholic churches, Mrs Bruce from St. John's Presbyterian, Mr Clive Bennet from the Council and Mr John McDonald from the Board of Trade."

"Most of you know me. I'm Bob Brooks for the Kinsmen Club; our president Mr Beach is presently at a meeting with the mayor, so he could not be here."

"The aim of this meeting is simply to get everyone on the same page regarding the needs and the efforts needed to get through this community crisis and help those most in need," he continued.

"Currently, we have thirty-six families who lost their houses or apartments, and 17 have nothing. The Kinsmen will staff a special fire relief bureau at the Town Hall to investigate the destitution.

"In addition, as a group, we need to reach out to all within our various organizations for donations of furniture, clothing, cooking utensils and other essentials."

Clive Bennet from the Council said, "We have reached out to landlords to see if they can provide rooms and housing, preferably at low rents, given that the breadwinners for many of the displaced families are now unemployed. We may, however, need to provide relief in the short term."

"The churches have opened their facilities and reached out to those in need," said Mary before being interrupted by Mr MacDonald from the Board of Trade.

"We need businesses rebuilt and financial help; those still standing need to get cleaned up, the stock sorted, and compensation for any losses," said MacDonald.

"Excuse me, Mr MacDonald, but people come before things," said Mary. I also understand the need there, but take the Bough family for example, husband, wife and eight kids spent the night in an open shed.

"No more than a neighbour's chicken coop. They only have the clothes on their back. Mr Bough is jobless, the relief committee provided food and clothing, but they should be a priority."

"Mayor Horovitz already said that rebuilding will start soon. Work will go first to those who lost their place of work due to the fire; we need to help people in the transition," said Elizabeth.

Everyone agreed, and each group left with their marching orders. The three ladies spoke for a few minutes outside the Club, feeling confident this could be done.

Chapter 4

The soundtrack of Cornwall was big band and swing, and this was no sleepy town. Its heartbeat was the waterfront, and the whistles from the factories signalled the start of the day. Hundreds made their way to the factories. In the east end, there were the Dundas and Canada Cotton Mills and Courtaulds, the Stormont Mill in the centre, and the Howard Smith Paper Mills in the west. Women worked in the sorting rooms, and men on the factory floors. Ships lined up at the canal's east end on their way to markets. After the morning rush, everything settled until it started again at the end of the day with the mass exodus of workers.

On Wednesday morning, Elizabeth opened the office, walked into a sunlit room, and was thankful the fire had spared this part of the street. She had never expected to one day own her own business, but it gave her a sense of purpose and pride. She had bought most of the furniture from her last tenant, a retired insurance agent. Her only extravagance had been a card catalogue unit with all the small drawers, like what they had in libraries.

She couldn't resist buying it from a local auction. The system appealed to her sense of organisation, and she used the cards to keep track of assignments, contacts, and details that could prove handy.

She had initially placed her desk by the window overlooking Pitt Street, but the distraction was too much. She found herself spending most of her day looking out. So now, her desk was between the windows, with her back to them, still providing lots of light for work. You walked into the office facing her, or more appropriately, Frank Lefebvre, and another desk was at the opposite corner. Beside the door was a coat rack where she placed a man's hat and jacket, holding the pretence that her boss came in regularly.

Mid-morning, Elizabeth decided to contact A.G. Drew.

"Mr Drew, this is Mrs Grant. After discussing your situation with Mr Lefebvre, he decided to take your case. Unfortunately, he is still away for a few days, but to get a head start, I was wondering if you could let me know when the time, date and location for the next meeting of your historical society?" asked Elizabeth.

"That is great news, Mrs Grant. I look forward to closing this affair and getting my book returned. Our next meeting is tomorrow evening," said Mr Drew.

"I wonder if you could introduce me. I want to enquire about Miss Smith and get a better picture of her from others that might know her," proposed Elizabeth.

"Well, it is Thursday at 6:30 at the Morrisburg public library, in one of the board rooms. Are you familiar with the location, Mrs Grant?"

"Yes, I know where it is, and I have transportation. It might be an idea to introduce me as a friend of your wife, someone interested in history; it might make things easier. I will see you then," said Elizabeth as she hung up.

Opening a new case was always exciting for Elizabeth, a challenge for her mind in fact-finding and resolution. However, this time she had a strange feeling that all might not be what it seemed.

Peter came in just before lunch, and she was glad to see him because they had a couple of cases to work on. Unfortunately, the fire had strained everyone's resources, and investigations had been contracted out.

"Hi, Aunt Liz, look what I have here," exclaimed Peter. He was holding a tiny screaming fur ball, more like fluffy charcoal than anything resembling a kitten.

"Mr Warner gave it to me when I went by. It came out of the rubble after the fire. I'm not sure what colour it is; it's more soot than fur right now.

"Mr Warner suggested I bring it over to you, adding that you might like company. I think Mr Warner is sweet on you, Aunt Liz!"

"I don't know about that, but that tiny kitten needs help. I'm not sure if I want to keep it, but let's feed it first, and then we can see," said Elizabeth, with a slight objection but already considering this kitten hers.

"What should we call it?"

"I can see "Dusty" might be a good match," suggested Peter.

"Dusty, it is, then. I have work for you, Peter. A postal investigator in Ottawa sent in the first case. They have received numerous complaints about non-deliveries of parcels in this area.

"It is Reginald McGillis, twenty-one and employed by Joseph Burns, who had the contract from the postal service for parcel delivery," explained Elizabeth.

"I could follow him discretely to see if anything is out of sorts. Can I borrow your car?" asked Peter.

"Absolutely; see over a few days if he returns with anything he can't deliver. He must be storing or hiding them somewhere. I'm not sure if he realises that the postal service takes this very seriously, and it could lead to jail time for theft," said Elizabeth.

"Let me know what you find, and I can report on it. Ottawa can then decide what to do about it after."

"And what are you working on, Aunt Liz?"

"A stolen book if you can imagine. And tomorrow night, I'm off to a historical society meeting in Morrisburg to start the investigation. So ok, let us see if we can find a place for Dusty to rest.

"That should be interesting," said Peter. As he walked out of the office, he considered telling Mr Warner that the kitten had found a home, giving him an opening for a follow-up.

"I might have a future as a matchmaker," he said to himself.

What to wear to a Morrisburg historical society meeting? Evenings in August were nice and warm, and Morrisburg being waterfront, there was always a breeze. She was no slave to fashion, but not a fan of the grandmother look either. She opted for a blouse and skirt in blue tones. Back when she used to live in Ottawa, her social life, often to support her husband's career, had been more active. He mostly approved of her choices, but one point of discussion was always her shoes. There she would not compromise. Unlike many women, she didn't like shoes. They suited one purpose only and had to be comfortable before anything else.

A hat was a must, which was unfortunate because she didn't think hats suited her. Since she had been in Cornwall and friends with Mary, her collection had grown. She was learning how to choose the ones that suited the shape of her face. Mary adored hats, and pieces from the best stores in Montreal and Europe supplemented her collection of suitable daywear.

After her husband died in a car crash, Elizabeth didn't think she would drive again. Then, they had a large and heavy Studebaker that was totalled in the accident. Once in Cornwall, she could walk everywhere and take the bus or train as needed. However, she did find that trips out of town, in and around the Counties, just for business were more difficult. So finally, she gave in and bought a used 1930 Ford Coupe.

She will never forget that shopping experience. She wasn't that knowledgeable about used cars, so she looked at newspaper ads to get an idea of prices. A nice thing about living in a small town, is that you always get references and gossip about local business owners. Friends had recommended Warner's Garage, on Second Street East, just past the King George Hotel. Before going there, though, she thought she would also look at another dealership just west of Warner's to get a better idea of prices.

She entered Foster's Garage and looked around for a while before a gentleman came over to her and asked, "Are you waiting for your husband, madam?"

To which Elizabeth replied, "No, it's just me."

The salesman found it hard to hide his disappointment, but nevertheless, he pursued. Finally, he introduced himself and asked whom he was addressing.

"What colour would you be looking for, Mrs Grant?"

"Since I'm looking for a used model, I am not set on a particular colour but would be looking for a small model in good condition, probably just a few years old."

He took her over to a two-door that didn't look in great shape and showed her the interior on the passenger side. "You will notice a huge glove compartment, very convenient."

"Can I look under the hood?" asked Elizabeth. She knew enough to be able to spot a dirty engine, worn belts and any leak.

"And why would you want to do that, Madam?" asked the salesman.

"Well, because it's a used car, and I would like to know what I'm getting," replied an exasperated Elizabeth.

"Can I take it for a test drive?"

At this point, she didn't really care about the car but just wanted to see what he would do next. As expected, he agreed to a test drive, provided he did all the driving. Elizabeth walked over to Warner's Garage a minute or so after that.

By now, she was frustrated, and her expectation of intelligent car-buying conversation was very low. Harry Warner saw Elizabeth walk in and remembered seeing her at various community events. He didn't get many women in his dealership, but business is business.

"Hello, Mrs Grant, nice to see you. How may I help you today?" Harry asked.

"I'm looking for a small used car, in good shape, maybe a couple of years old."

She proceeded to tell him what sort of car they had before and her need for something easy to handle. He made a few recommendations, but she seemed to know what she was looking for. He took her over to a nice 1930 Ford Coupe and showed her the interior.

"Would you like to take it for a test drive? You can tell me what you think." Harry set up a test licence plate for her and sat on the passenger's side.

"Thank you, that's one step above the competition!" said Elizabeth.

"There's the competition?" smiled Harry.

"A lady never tells."

She settled on the car, and the service was excellent, a bit above and beyond when Harry delivered the car himself, including a full tank of gas. Her sister-in-law teased her about a particular interest behind that service. Elizabeth protested but was touched by the attention, which she didn't encourage, but appreciated. A woman her age could always use a compliment or two.

The trip from Cornwall to Morrisburg was about 35 minutes and a lovely outing along the King's Highway 2, taking in all the villages on the front. Elizabeth was now becoming a "local" as she knew that all the villages on the waterfront were referred to as "the front."

When the family visited her husband's relatives in Cornwall, they often drove to the head of Sheek Island for a Sunday picnic and swim. The girls loved it, and it was full of other children to play with. There were rumours again about the expansion of the canal system and hydro project with the States. Elizabeth didn't know all the details, but it meant significant changes for all the villages along the shoreline.

The Morrisburg library was easy to find, and many people were coming for the historical society meeting. Mr Drew told her that a presentation was always first, followed by the society's agenda and discussions. Elizabeth thought she could stay for the meet and greet and presentation and leave before the member's business started.

A.G. Drew was waiting for her at the door. "Good evening, Mrs Grant; this is my wife, Jennie. We can go in for a coffee before the presentation, and I will make the introductions."

Elizabeth noticed the sign at the entrance for tonight's discussion on the Fenian Raids by John Harper. Oddly enough, she had come across a bit of that history when she first started at the Department of Justice. A. G. Drew introduced her to members of the Society as a friend of Jennie's with an interest in local history.

"Well, Mrs Drew, you know about my work trying to find the missing book. What was your impression of Miss Smith?" started Elizabeth.

"Please call me Jennie. Don't take this the wrong way, but I'm not sure he should go through the expense of an investigator, but this book means a lot to him.

"Josephine Smith seemed equal to the task of getting a value on it, but then she started the run around about giving it back."

"Did she find out anything about it?" asked Elizabeth.

"In October last year, she sent us a postcard from Montreal saying a priest had confirmed it was written in old Scots and that she would secure more opinions.

"A.G. had given her the book in September, as I recall. About a month later, when she was back in Morrisburg, she came to our house, and he asked her for the book. At that time, she said it was in Merrickville," stated Jennie.

"Did she mention the book's whereabouts with anyone else while she was in town," asked Elizabeth.

"A friend of my husband's, William Lawson, also met her. Let me get him for you,"

Jennie waved to a handsome gentleman near the coffee table.

"Good evening, I am Ernest Lawson, a barrister from Chesterville, and my ancestors fought the Fenians, so here I am," laughed Lawson.

"A.G. quietly mentioned your agency was helping with the book matter. Anything I can do to help?"

"Jennie mentioned you met Miss Smith?" asked Elizabeth, thinking there must be a Mrs Lawson in the vicinity.

"Yes, we met her at the Windsor, the hotel where she was staying. It was back in November.

"Drew was looking to get his book back, and she told us the book was packed in a case and not easily accessible. That seemed odd to me. She knew she was coming to town, so why not bring the book?

"She did say the book was in Merrickville and that she would return it later," confirmed Lawson.

"She said her home was in Merrickville, but Drew tracked her in various places in Eastern Ontario and the States. That's when the run around started, I feel."

"Thank you very much for your help, Mr Lawson," Elizabeth said as she put her coffee cup on the nearby table. "It seems we are about to find out about your ancestors," as the door opened to the board room, and they were ushered in.

Elizabeth was happy with the outcome of the evening. She managed to learn more about Miss Smith. After the presentation, she excused herself and told A.G. Drew that she would fill in Mr Lefebvre and move the investigation along. On the drive home, she replayed the conversations in her mind, and she couldn't help thinking that she had heard the name Josephine Smith before. Then, as she drove past Dickinson's Landing it hit her! The Fenians, that was the connection!

Chapter 5

Department of Justice, East Block, Ottawa, 1903

Elizabeth settled at her desk for the day ahead. The typing pool on the third floor was a large open room with rows of desks for the typists and three larger desks at the front for the supervisors. Each morning, at the stroke of nine, files were put in the inbox on the left, starting the rhythm of typewriter keys for the rest of the day. Once a file was completed, it moved to the outbox on the right, and clerks would come by and pick them up for review and filing.

The key to success here was accuracy and speed, and Elizabeth tried her best. The reward was eventually moving out of the typing pool and becoming a clerk or even a secretary. The work was routine, but the blossoming of friendships she made it fun.

"Miss Richards? Elizabeth? Would you come by my desk before the lunch break, please?" asked Miss Jones, the head of the department.

Elizabeth nodded without slowing down, wondering what it was all about. Her work has been good lately, so she didn't expect a reprimand, although one could never be sure. Finally, at a quarter to twelve, Elizabeth walked over to the front of the room, knowing that her friends' eyes were on her.

"Elizabeth, I must say your work has been excellent, and your transcriptions are accurate," said Miss Jones.

"We need someone for a temporary assignment to replace a leave of absence in the investigation branch on the second floor. Would you be interested?"

"Very much so, Miss Jones," said Elizabeth with relief. The supervisor did not praise lightly, so it was all good.

"You can start tomorrow. After that, you will probably work with Mr William Grant for two weeks," explained Miss Jones.

"Thank you, I will tidy up my desk at the end of the day. Thank you for the opportunity, Miss Jones."

The lunchtime bell rang, and the room fell silent as everyone went out. Elizabeth grabbed her bag and ran outside to sit in the sun with her friends.

"So? Are you in trouble? Why were you called up?" asked Sue as the other girl laughed.

"No, I always do excellent work, don't you know?" replied Elizabeth.

"It's an assignment for a couple of weeks."

"Oh, where are you going? Not with Mr Perkins, I hope. He's always in need of new clerks and a little too friendly if you know what I mean," commented Stella.

"Investigation, with William Grant. I don't think I've heard anything about him," said Elizabeth cheerfully.

"Lucky you, he's new and quite a looker," said Sue.

"I wouldn't mind an assignment there!"

"No worries, I'm looking for a promotion, not a husband," laughed Elizabeth.

The following day Elizabeth made her way to William Grant's office on the second floor. She introduced herself to the secretary, who took her in to see Mr Grant. She thought he was young for someone with his own office. Sue was right, he was handsome, but she mostly liked his voice and calm demeanour.

"Miss Richards, thank you for your assistance. But unfortunately, I'm afraid it will have to be a very short learning curve as we are in the middle of an investigation, and my clerk had an accident and will be away for a while," said William.

Elizabeth nodded and opened her notepad, curious to see what she would be working on.

"What do you know of the Fenians, Miss Richards?" asked William.

"Very little, I'm afraid. I remember learning in school about some raids and a group of Irish trying to put pressure on England by invading and disturbing the colonies?" attempted Elizabeth.

"Partially right, Miss Richards."

William explained that the Fenian Brotherhood was founded in New York City in 1858 as an Irish Republican organisation. The Brotherhood aimed to end British rule in Ireland. In America, they sold bonds in the name of the Irish Republic, and thousands of Irish immigrants bought them. The funds' purchased large quantities of arms for raids into Canada. The plan was to seize the transportation network, forcing the British to exchange Ireland's freedom for the province of Canada. The Fenians had intelligence that some Irish Canadians supported this plan.

"So, closer to us, the St. Lawrence Valley was of interest to them for the canals and bridges," said William.

"On our side, a Militia was raised, and the invasion attempt failed. Things quieted down, but the group was still active, and the Canadian government kept an eye on their developments.

"After 1867, the Clan Na Gael was formed, and bombing raids took place in England. Fortunately, with the aid of informants, most attempts stalled.

"Their aspirations never really died, and now, with politics in Europe, some feel they may seek support elsewhere, with alliances that could threaten Europe. So, Canada is ideally positioned to provide intelligence to the British. And that, Miss Richards, is our role," ended William.

"I see," said Elizabeth, as she tried to absorb all the information and its broader meaning as to her new work.

"Of course, anything you hear or see while working here is highly confidential. Fortunately, your file shows that you already had the security clearance," mentioned William.

"Your desk will be beside my secretary, and you can ask her for anything you need. You will mostly deal with correspondence and reports from our people in the field."

The first week just flew by. Many of the letters that came in were handwritten, and copies were made, dated, and numbered. Referrals of documents from one department to another, Justice, Governor General, Secretary of State, and 10 Downing Street. Elizabeth thought it was fascinating, and she enjoyed working with William. She was impressed by how many things he could deal with simultaneously. It was fast-paced, and he expected accuracy, but he was always supportive.

The second week was hectic. A US government agent from Philadelphia came in for a meeting, and telegrams were transferred from one department to another. Elizabeth had missed lunch with the girls and often had to grab a quick bite with William to go over what needed to be done. Not that she minded; she got to know him better. She learned that he was raised in Cornwall and trained as a lawyer and was glad of the position with the Department of Justice. His job was to see if any dealings and intelligence findings broke any laws of the country.

"Miss Richards, can you come into my office, please?" asked William.

"I have just received this telegram from one of our operatives in Omaha, Nebraska. Can you make copies and send them up the chain, please?"

Elizabeth took the paper and went directly to her desk. It said:

Glan Na Gael meeting in Omaha Friday, September 11th. Moving towards contact with Germany with support. J.S.

Two days later, a letter came in from the contact in Omaha, and William called her in and handed her the letter.

"Same drill with this one, copy and forward. When you are done, please come back in. We will need to plan to move our contact out of the States for a while," said William.

"She lives in Merrickville but has sisters in Omaha and Philadelphia. This has made it easy for her to get back and forth unsuspectedly. The link to the Clan comes from her cousin in Omaha.

The letter read:

Dear Sir,

Through having given you notice of the meeting in Omaha, I believe the Clan Na Gael might be aware of my information. My mail has been opened in more than one instance, and I fear the coffee prepared for me was poisoned, and a shot intended for me just escaped my mother by six inches.

Please advise,

Josephine Smith

On Friday, Elizabeth realised it was her last day with William. She was told the permanent clerk would be back to work. She thought about wearing something special but didn't want to be silly about it. So, she took more care than usual and borrowed her sister's more fashionable shoes.

She knew some of the clerks didn't like the temp girls leaving their desks in a mess, so she cleared everything and went into William's office.

"Anything for me this morning, Mr Grant?" asked Elizabeth.

"Hi, oh yes, we will move Miss Smith out of the US for a while. We need to arrange for a quick transfer to her home in Merrickville.

"Her usefulness to us might be over. I want to thank you for your work in the last two weeks. It means we won't be working together anymore," said William.

"You could always ask for me if you ever need a clerk," hinted Elizabeth.

"Actually, no, I wouldn't…" paused William.

"I would rather you accompany me to the opening of the Central Canada Exhibition this Saturday. Would you?"

"That would be lovely," smiled Elizabeth.

"Oh, by the way, I like the shoes," grinned William.

Chapter 6

Cornwall, August 1933

Elizabeth jumped out of her daydream and went over what she remembered. That's where she came across Josephine Smith! If this was the case, then she was savvier than Mr Drew would expect.

"Hi, Aunt Liz, how's Dusty?" asked Peter as he walked in.

"Just fine; he is a black and grey tabby now that I cleaned him up. Any progress on the case of the missing parcel?" asked Elizabeth.

"Yes!" exclaimed Peter. "I had to follow him for a few days, but eventually, he slipped up.

"I could see him loading his delivery van in the morning, and then one afternoon, he drove off early back to the farm of his employer Mr Burns.

"He backed up the delivery van, took mail bags, into the barn, and then by the sawdust heap in the yard."

"Do you think Mr Burns is in on it?" said Elizabeth.

"I'm not sure, but he wasn't at home when McGillis went there," explained Peter.

"Thank you and let me know your hours. I will report to the postal investigator in Ottawa and let him decide what happens," said Elizabeth.

"I don't need the car this weekend. If you want to see Susan, you can borrow it."

"Thanks, Aunt Liz, that would be great; you're the best," praising as he kissed her cheek.

She jotted down all the information on the postal case and would drop it off at the post office this afternoon. The mail ran twice daily, so Ottawa should get it on Monday. She made sure to include an invoice for services.

Now her mind was bubbling with all the information she had gathered about Josephine Smith. But what of the book? Where was it now? She wished someone was there to bounce off ideas. That's when she missed her husband. There was, however, never an occasion desperate enough for her to consider starting a whole new relationship. Her marriage had been good and stable, and she appreciated this. She had seen plenty of drama with her parents and didn't go looking for it in her own life. She opted to call her friend Mary. A stop at Fullerton's Tearoom would be a nice break.

❧

Mary had agreed to meet her at Fullerton's on Saturday afternoon. Elizabeth quickly filled her in on her progress.

"Now I'm wondering where the book is?" said Elizabeth.

"If Josephine Smith shipped it to Philadelphia as she claims, it's almost impossible to confirm. Even going through customs, the shipping manifest is unlikely to list the valuable Mary Queen of Scots prayer book, is it?"

"Well, do you know if there is a market for this sort of artefact in Philadelphia?" suggested Mary.

"With the economy right now, it might be difficult, although there might be more value in antiques and art than in the fluctuating currencies."

Mary might have a point there. As an artist, Mary had trained in Paris and was part of the Montreal art scene before returning to Cornwall. She had stayed in touch with many in the field and had good contacts in Ottawa.

"Would you know anyone who would tell me how to get such a book on the market if it became available?" asked Elizabeth.

"I just might. I'm in Ottawa next week for a meeting. I will see and let you know," replied Mary.

"Now, I need to learn about the legal aspect. Who owns the book?

"We can't claim ownership even if we find it on the market in Philadelphia. One would need to be able to prove it was stolen. There is a lawyer friend of William I could ask how we could make this stick. Anyone who paid good money for it would be unlikely to return it without proof," surmised Elizabeth.

"Easy, you'll just have to catch her red-handed," laughed Mary.

Chapter 7

Elizabeth was glad Peter dropped by the office early before his classes. There were a few things to go over before her trip to Ottawa. The visit would combine family time with a few meetings about the Drew/Smith case. Mary had arranged an appointment with a well-known Ottawa bookseller, and she would meet with a colleague and friend of her husband, a lawyer still at the Department of Justice. Elizabeth was hoping their answers might give her a sense of direction.

As Peter walked in, Elizabeth noticed he was dressed more formally than usual, looking quite the businessman.

"Anything important going on today? You look ready to make a good impression?" she asked.

"My training is ending, and I have an interview for an apprenticeship in accounting with a local firm," replied Peter. "My grades are good, but I want to look the part."

"I'm sure you will do fine, and I can always give you a character reference if they need one. Your work here has been great," said Elizabeth.

"Thanks. Talking about work, has anything further come in on the case I was working on, you know, the undelivered parcels?" asked Peter.

"As a matter of fact, I did get an update. They've arrested Reginald McGillis. They found two mail sacks with fifty-nine parcels inside, hidden in the sawdust.

"And that's not all, they found more in his delivery van, under a horse blanket, and around the barn where you saw him.

"Did he have anything to say for himself?" asked Peter.

"Nothing substantial," replied Elizabeth.

"He said he had been too busy to deliver them and would get to them later, but some had been in the barn for months. Mr St Laurent, the postmaster, said he paid by the hour and that Reginald was allowed the time needed to do the deliveries.

"It's too bad, Reginald just lost himself a good job, and a police record won't help him down the road," said Peter.

Elizabeth told him about her plans for the coming week, including her trip to Ottawa. She said that Frank Lefebvre was still away. She was hoping Peter would drop by to feed Dusty. She also had more work for him if he was available.

"With this placement interview and your course ending, will you still have some time for work at the agency?" asked Elizabeth.

"I don't want to throw too many things at you if you need time to study for the final exams."

"I can fit it all in, Aunt Liz," said Peter. "You and Mr Lefebvre have been so good at giving me work around my schedule, and you're still my number one! But, of course, many things I do for you, like surveillance, can be done at different times, so we're all good for now."

"Ok, thank you for that," said Elizabeth.

"I can't see training anyone else for now, and we can discuss everything as we go along the rest of the year. I have another case, a fraud on pension funds."

Elizabeth explained, "The Department of Pensions and National Health asked us to find out about Peter Rochon, who lives in town. He applied for a pension for himself and his wife, but he does not seem to have a wife or anyone else living with him now."

"So, you want me to look into it, see who comes and goes out of his house?" asked Peter.

"Yes, perhaps ask around, discretely, neighbours, that sort of thing," said Elizabeth.

"If there is a wife, there would be laundry, shopping, and visitors. If we can confirm the suspicions, the Department can take over from there and save time on the groundwork."

"I'm off to Ottawa for the next few days. Ask your mother if she needs me to get anything for her while I'm there, will you?" said Elizabeth.

Chapter 8

It was the end of summer, and Ottawa was getting back to business. Walking down Wellington Street, Elizabeth realised she missed living and working in the city. The formality of the Parliamentary buildings, the Chateau Laurier Hotel's architecture, and the Canal's ingenuity always impressed her. She was born and raised over on Bank Street, above her father's shop.

Her father was a shy and quiet man who repaired shoes, worked leather, and was the neighbourhood handyman. When times were tough, he would barter repairs for goods and staples. Her parents had married late in life, and she was their only child. Just as her father had been even-tempered, her mother was the opposite. She was plagued with bouts of depression that had brought a greyness into their lives. There were days when her mother did not get out of bed. Her father did his best to manage the house and the shop, and Elizabeth took care of herself. Coming home from school, there was very little she could do to lift her mother's spirits, so she found refuge in her father's shop.

Elizabeth was fifteen when her mother passed away. A year later, her father re-married a widowed shopkeeper with a large, noisy brood. Elizabeth was welcomed into the fold, and the veil had lifted. Her father smiled again. Both her father and stepmother had long passed away, but the smell of the leather shop was forever linked to her memories of him.

Mary had put her in touch with a bookseller on Sparks Street, James Hope & Sons, who specialised in religious books. They were also bookbinders and printers. There she hoped to learn more about Drew's book, the why and how one could profit from it. The imposing nine-storey building at 61 Sparks Street was aptly named "Bible House", and the mahogany and bronze entryway added to the pomp and circumstance.

"Good day, Madam. How may I help you?" asked the young clerk.

"I'm here to see Mr Hope. I have an appointment this morning," replied Elizabeth.

The clerk led her to an office in the back, where a well-dressed man in his mid-thirties motioned her to take a seat. Elizabeth thought he did not look the part at all, not someone you would call a bookworm or remotely associate with a "Bible House." His stance and frame would be more at home on a sporting field. She reminded herself not to judge a book by its cover!

"I'm Mrs Elizabeth Grant, I was referred by my friend Mary Randolph. Thank you so much for taking the time to see me," said Elizabeth.

"It's my pleasure, and I'm John Hope. Mary told me about the item in question, and I was intrigued.

"Both our mothers went to the same boarding school in Montreal and remained in touch. I played some tennis with Mary and her brother Harold; both are friends of mine as well.

"I work for a private investigator, and this case has come along; I was asked to find out more about the book at the centre of this investigation. It is rare and has not been returned. The owner thinks it's been sent out of the country for sale." Elizabeth proceeded to fill him in on what she knew so far.

"Did the owner, this Mr Drew, tell you what the book looks like, its binding or cover?" asked Hope.

"Well, he said the paper was different than what we see today, more like fabric, and the binding was sturdier, like boards. However, he did say a priest's name was written on the flyleaf, a Father Conificus, I believe," replied Elizabeth.

"That name does not mean anything to me, but that book block would be right for one printed in the 1500s," said Hope.

"What I am debating, though, is the language in which the book was written. He said Old English, and Miss Smith said she had it identified as Old Scots? That seems unlikely to me, and it might have been misidentified, either the language or the subject matter.

"You see, so far, all the prayer books associated with Mary Queen of Scots were written in Latin with one exception written in Latin and French.

This is because the language of religion at that time was Latin.

"Also, you say he acquired it from a flea market. That seems even stranger because anyone with this type of book would recognize it as rare right away and unlikely to part with it in that way."

"There is also the book's origin and provenance," Elizabeth said. "How would such a rare book make it into this country, mostly unnoticed?"

"It may be easier in Ottawa than in other locations because of the comings and goings of diplomats and government officials from around the world. Even a stolen book could circulate easily until it was time for a sale, and they're all cash transactions," said Hope.

"In the rare book trade, we keep a keen eye on ownership and provenance. Selling stolen items, for example, could ruin the reputation of an auction house, and such an illicit deal would need to be made in private."

"But say it was stolen in the first place, wouldn't it be reported?" asked Elizabeth.

"Good question," said Hope. "Normally, there are ownership markings, a stamp, an embossed seal, a number, with libraries for sure.

"Even private owners have their system. But rare books get stolen, even from national and university libraries. Often an inside job, quick money from unscrupulous collectors.

"More extensive libraries seldom do a complete inventory, and it can be years before a missing book is reported."

"So, what about value? How much could such a book go for, in your opinion?" asked Elizabeth.

"That varies, but for example, the Gutenberg Bible sold for $106,000 US in 1926. Of course, after the crash of '29, the rare book market also plummeted. Still, there are avid collectors out there.

"The antiquarian book trade between Britain and the US was strong, and the exportation was never regulated. When demand exceeds supply, prices rise, and the criminal element can become creative."

"So where would you go to buy or sell at the best price?" asked Elizabeth.

"Certainly New York, but Philadelphia has grown with new auction houses," concluded Hope.

"Thank you very much for your time, Mr Hope. This has been most informative," said Elizabeth.

"Let me know if there is anything else I can do for you, and please give my best to Mary."

Elizabeth then proceeded to her next appointment on Wellington Street. Edward Rushton had been a colleague and friend of her husband, both working at the Department of Justice. The two men had a strong friendship, but Elizabeth and Edward's wife, Julie, never managed to move beyond small talk about cooking and kids.

"Hi Edward, it's so nice to see you!" said Elizabeth. "How are Julie and the boys?"

"Oh, you know Julie, always busy with the grandkids now and the house. She lost interest in me the minute the children were born," he said sadly.

"And you? I've heard you moved to Cornwall after…."

"Yes, it was hard to sell the house, but I couldn't go on like that. William was gone so quickly. After he died, I kept waiting for him to come home at the end of the day," explained Elizabeth.

"I needed a change to get me to live again.

"Now I have settled in Cornwall. I have work and friends, but still close enough for the family to stay connected.

"I work for a private detective agency; we have even hired my nephew, the oldest boy of Bella, William's sister.

"A detective agency, well, that doesn't surprise me," Edward exclaimed.

"It's so You! I remember the three of us going over cases from the Department. You could always see the links."

"Thanks, Edward, my asking for a meeting was not totally by coincidence, actually," said Elizabeth.

"We have a case right now, and I could use your legal input; I'm at a loss here."

Elizabeth went on to fill him in on all the details about the Drew/Smith case and the mysterious book. Edward was as intrigued as he was glad to help.

"There is another thing, and you might have to look into this," suggested Elizabeth.

"When I worked with William at the Department, we had contact with an operative who reported on the Fenian Brotherhood and Clan Na Gael.

"Her name was Josephine Smith, and I think it might be the same woman. So, there is a connection there, living in the same area, name, and so on."

"Wow, that was a long time ago," said Edward.

"I'll see what I can find out. Just write down where I can reach you."

❧

While in Ottawa, Elizabeth stayed with her daughter Margaret, named after William's mother. Margaret (Margie) and her family lived in the east end, off Saint Laurent, close to where her husband, James, worked at the National Research Council as an engineer. Margie looked very much like her mother, with the same curly brown hair. Margie married young to her high school sweetheart, and they now had twin daughters, six years old.

Elizabeth's youngest daughter Muriel would join them for dinner, squeezing in a visit with her mother between myriad other activities on her calendar. The two sisters got along well but could not be more different. Margie had been an easy child to raise, while Muriel had to stretch the rules like rubber bands. No doubt Muriel had been the cause of her husband's prematurely grey hair. She was in the editing department of *The Ottawa Journal*, where she hoped one day to become a reporter. She was single and lived downtown with a group of girls from the newspaper.

Muriel arrived at 5:30 pm, always in a rush, greeted by the twins who adored her. She was wearing women's pants, the wide-leg slacks, her light hair in a fashionable wave. Elizabeth could not help but notice how much she looked like her father.

"Oh, I love those slacks," said Elizabeth.

"You should try them, mother. Everyone is wearing them now," said Muriel.

"I don't think it's my style, or Cornwall's for that matter, for a woman my age."

"Well, that's the thing, isn't it? You don't want to be "your age." You have a good figure; lead the Cornwall fashion scene," laughed Muriel.

Everyone gathered at the table and exchanged news, and the lively conversation was something Elizabeth had missed. They wanted to know about her work at the agency, so she told a few funny stories, keeping it light to not worry them.

After dinner, Muriel had to leave early, so Elizabeth and Margie, took Grace and Agnes to the park, and as they sat down on the bench, Elizabeth could feel the conversation turning towards "The" talk. The recurring chat about her decision to move away.

"So, are you ready to come back to Ottawa now?" asked Margie.

"We miss you. You've proven your point; it's been three years now. I know it's not the money, Dad left you enough to be comfortable."

"Do we need to go over this again, Margie? I'm happy with my life right now."

"Are we not enough?"

The question gave Elizabeth a jolt, "Of course, you are enough, and I'm sorry if I ever made you feel otherwise.

"For years I was Mrs William Grant, and I loved being a wife and mother, but I want to play more than just a supporting role in my own life."

Just then, Elizabeth thought, I want my name on the office door.

"What I mean to say is that there should be some manner of choice. We shouldn't lose ourselves in the role of wife and mother; we can be more than one thing," she added as she hugged her daughter.

"I'm pregnant," said Margie.

"Oh, this is wonderful news. I don't have a grandson yet; it will be so much fun.

"I will help, once the baby comes, I can come up or take the girls with me for a couple of weeks. We'll have a great time, and it will make things easier for you. I am here for you; never doubt that."

They all walked back to the house, chatting about baby names and explaining the roles of big sisters to the twins.

Chapter 9

The next morning back in Cornwall, the early call took Elizabeth by surprise as she was getting ready to go to the office.

"Morning, Elizabeth, it's Edward Rushton. I need to see you as soon as possible. I have some information about this case you are working on. We might have to put you back on the payroll. Your boss might need to know as well."

"Are you coming down today?" asked Elizabeth. "I can clear my schedule whenever you need."

"Yes, I should be there later today; see you then," said Edward.

Elizabeth wondered what it was all about, and if the Department of Justice was going to be involved, it might be time for her to come clean about Frank Lefebvre. Time would tell.

Edward arrived at the office mid-morning and went on to explain the situation.

"You were right about the connection to Josephine Smith and the Fenians but, as for AG Drew, he is a random element," said Edward.

"The book was stolen from the National Library of Scotland; it was an inside job. A senior librarian stole several books over time and fenced them at an auction house under a false name."

"The Fenians recruited the librarian to convert some of the stolen books to cash. The transaction was to be made in Canada because of the ease of access. At customs, he had an unfortunate heart attack and died onsite.

"The Department of Justice, which had been following this delivery, could not prove anything, but no books were found with the deceased, and only two customs officers were at work that evening: AG Drew and George Seymour. We decided to keep tabs on both, but Drew became the main suspect."

Edward continued, "Given his location and interest, we decided to call upon Josephine again and re-activate her as an informant. Of course, as an antiquarian and historian, she was to befriend him, hoping he would confide and show her the book.

"But, of course, it was beyond expectations that he would give it to her, hoping she would put a price on it, who knows, maybe find a buyer.

"Soon after she "borrowed" the book, we lost track of her, and so did Drew. We had no clue until you came to me with your stolen book investigation. So now Smith is either running or hiding and if so, from whom?

"Did she decide to keep the book for herself? Are the Fenians also tracking her down? You are our only lead now. You already have Drew's ear, and you know the area. Are you interested in helping us?"

"Sure, but what is your priority?" asked Elizabeth.

"There is a bigger picture here, yes?"

"Smith and Drew are small players," replied Edward.

"We have no interest in Drew and limited interest in Smith, only as far as her having connections with the Fenians. The book is a means to an end, finding out the instigators. It's a small, resolute faction, but we fear those who make alliances of convenience with those even more radical. Canada, Britain, and the US are on the same page with this."

"You know that when you worked for William, some things he feared did happen.

"Clan Na Gael in America did request from Germany a shipload of ammunition, officers, machine guns, and the like in support of the 1916 Easter Rising in Ireland. They asked that a submarine escort accompany the boat and wanted 100,000 riffles, but only 20,000 were allocated. American intelligence spoiled the plans, and one of the organizers was executed for treason. Of course, Germany denied any involvement."

"William never said anything," said Elizabeth.

"No, he wouldn't have, but it was and still is a scary world. How about lunch while you consider all this?" asked Edward.

Glad for the pause, Elizabeth suggested walking up Pitt Street to the Royal York Café. The overhanging neon sign, checkered floor, and wooden booths presented normalcy in stark contrast to the devastation the fire had caused across the street.

"Wow," said Edward. "I read about the fire but didn't realize the extent of the decimated area."

"Yes, it left many people without homes or jobs," said Elizabeth.

"They are rebuilding, so it will get better. Lots of people looking for work right now, and many are coming in from the countryside to try and get hired. Priority in getting work on the rebuilding was given to those residents directly affected."

After a quiet lunch, Edward returned to the charge, "So, will you help us?"

"Yes, I will," replied Elizabeth.

"Now, from a national security point of view, we would much rather move this scenario to Canada," explained Edward.

"Of course, we could follow Josephine Smith and let her do the deal in Philadelphia, where the Fenians think they will get the most money for the book. But, if we do that, we only get the operatives on that side of the border.

"We need to get the Fenians' leadership in Canada. So, the book must come back here."

"I will follow up with Drew and see if he heard more from her. That should tell us where things stand," said Elizabeth.

"Great, we will keep in touch, and I will let you know who else is working the case for the Mounties. Do you want me to talk to your boss?"

"No, it's okay, he is away right now, but I explained everything, and he sent you a note.

> *Mr Rushton,*
>
> *Mrs Grant has kept me abreast of the recent developments in the peculiar case. I have made her available to help you in any way she can. She has my complete confidence in this matter.*
>
> *Regards,*
>
> *François Lefebvre*

"That's great," said Edward. "He sounds nice and has much respect for your work."

"He certainly does, and I don't know where he'd be without me," replied Elizabeth.

Chapter 10

The next morning in the office, Elizabeth tried to organize her thoughts and make sense of it all. Everything was coming at her full speed, and she needed Peter to help more than ever.

"Hi, Aunt Liz, keeping busy, I see," said Peter.

"Yes, I will fill you in on things coming in but first, how did your work on the Rochon case go?" asked Elizabeth.

"Does it look like he has a wife at home?"

"No, he doesn't and not for a while, from what I got from the next-door neighbour," said Peter.

"Your pointers were good, there was no woman's clothing on the line for laundry day, and while Mr Rochon was out, I pretended to have a delivery needing signature.

"The neighbour was more than willing to tell tales and told me there hadn't been a Mrs Rochon living there for at least two years. She left him."

"Good work Peter," said Elizabeth. I will send that in quickly to our Pensions contact, and they can do the rest."

"Now, there is, another case I'm working on. A federal case, very confidential, and I know I can count on you for that," continued Elizabeth.

"I must also tell you, at this point, that there is no Frank Lefebvre, no private investigator that owns the agency. I made it up, and I'm sorry for not telling you earlier. It's all just me."

"Oh, I knew that I figured it out a long time ago, Aunt Liz. I also understand why you did it."

"Thanks, it's all set then," said Elizabeth.

"How would you like to take a day trip to Merrickville? Take Susan with you if her parents agree or suggest taking her sister along.

"I need you to investigate a lady named Josephine Smith, who is from there. She authored a book, so perhaps the library might know her. You can say you are wondering about her work. Also, I need to know about her family. For instance, she has sisters in the States. So, anything could help at this stage."

"I can do that, and I will let you know straight away if I find something," said Peter.

"We will have to walk to Warner's Garage to pick up the car. There was a screeching noise when I started it, and I wanted to get it looked at before it got worse," said Elizabeth.

The garage was close by on Second Street, and when they entered, Harry Warner got up from his desk, rolled down his sleeves, and put on his jacket to greet them at the counter. He was in his late forties or early fifties, with black hair, curly and bushy, held in check by a recent haircut. He had deep brown eyes and a square face, with an air of no-nonsense about him.

"Good day Mrs Grant, hi Peter. Coming to get your car?" he said. "Let me get the paperwork.

"It's all fixed, only a minor problem with the starter belt, which we replaced. We also did a nice exterior wash for you, as long as it was in the shop," he said.

"Mrs Grant, have you heard of the Kinsmen Fundraising Dinner?"

Seeing where this conversation was going, Peter decided to look at some of the cars on the showroom floor.

Harry Warner persevered, "The Kinsmen Club started just this year, and I'm a member. We help in the community; we staffed a twenty-hour bureau to collect funds and necessities for the fire relief.

"The club is doing a fundraising dinner, I have a table for the garage, and there is an empty seat. Would you like to join me? You would know most of the wives there?"

Elizabeth did not expect this and had to do a quick balance sheet in her mind. Plusses, minuses, in each column for a yes or a no.

She finally said, "That would be nice; what day and time?"

Harry made a slight sigh of relief and said, "Friday, in two weeks, at the Cornwallis Hotel starts at 6:30 pm. Would you like me to pick you up?"

"It's very close, and I might be finishing work at the office around that time, so I can meet you there," Elizabeth said, trying to keep it casual. She paid the bill and gave the keys to Peter.

"You got a free wash, interesting," teased Peter.

With Peter on his way to Merrickville, Elizabeth decided to ring Mary and seek her help with this Fenian Brotherhood research, and she was best placed to know what happened locally.

"Hi Mary, I'm going to the library. I need some background information on the Fenian Brotherhood," Elizabeth said.

"Your local knowledge would help. Can I drop in afterwards, say early evening?"

"I will be home; mother will be visiting my aunt so that it will be quiet for a chat; looking forward to seeing you," said Mary.

Elizabeth walked on Second Street to the nearby library. It was overflowing with material, and she was likely to find something on the history of the Fenian movement. It seemed to her that links to the present day were weak, but she could be wrong.

Time flew by, and she was only interrupted by the librarian signalling that the doors would close in a few minutes. Mary's home was a block away on the same street. It was a stately house, two-storey red brick with a front porch the length of the façade. Mary had told her it was built for her parents when they married in 1897. Mary was sitting outside, reading, and enjoying this beautiful September evening.

"So, did you find what you needed at the library?" asked Mary.

"More or less," said Elizabeth.

"It's an overview, but I thought you could tell me about the local history. I know it is one of your favourite subjects."

"It was a long time ago, but we did see signs and threats of Fenian Raids here in Cornwall," said Mary.

"My grandfather was part of the militia raised at the time and received a Canada General Service Medal and a piece of land for it."

"So, this area was a strategic target because of the location, the canal, and the commerce routes to Toronto and the US?" asked Elizabeth.

"Yes, and train bridges all along the St. Lawrence. Fortunately, they were not successful, but the threats were there.

"Finally, in 1866, they arrested Michael Murphy and six others at Cornwall's train station. They were on their way to the States. The police confiscated weapons, ammunition, and money and were set for trial, but finally, they escaped. That was quite the saga."

"How so?" asked Elizabeth.

"Well, they were held at the County Jail on Water Street, by the waterfront. They had outside help, a tunnel was dug under the jail wall, and they escaped by boat to the United States.

"It was hours before anyone realized they had gone."

"How interesting, but that was long ago," Elizabeth said.

"Nothing more recent happened that you know of?"

"The Fenian Brotherhood became the Clan Na Gael in the US," explained Mary.

"In turn, they supported the Irish Republican Brotherhood, the 1916 Easter Rising, and the 1919 Irish War of Independence. American and Canadian money was sent over.

"I remember my father saying it was something like $100,000 sent to Ireland in the years before the Easter Rising."

"The Clan now seems to support the Irish Republican Army," added Mary.

"In 1900, there were unsuccessful attempts to blow up the Welland Canal, which sent militia to Cornwall because of fears it could also happen to the canal here."

"Mary, how do you know all these things?" asked Elizabeth.

"If all else fails, you could be a history teacher!"

"Both my grandfathers were in politics, as I told you, one in the militia against the raids, and my father was the county sheriff," she explained.

"As an only child, and likely a bit precocious, I took an interest, couldn't help it; it was all around me."

"It serves you well and helps me," said Elizabeth.

"I can't tell you everything, but it helps with a case I'm working on. On another matter, are you going to the Kinsmen Fundraising Dinner on Friday night?"

"Yes, mother and I will go. It's a fundraiser to help those affected by the fire. It's a slow recovery for some," said Mary.

"You are welcomed to join us if you want."

"Harry Warner asked me to sit at his table to make the eight," replied Elizabeth.

"So, a dinner date?"

"Not really; he's not picking me up or anything that formal. I'm just sitting at his table, filling in the last seat," said Elizabeth.

"I admire your logic, so he's winning you over by not trying too hard?" smiled Mary.

"Oh, give me a break!" added Elizabeth.

"Plus, I need a nice evening out. I have been so busy lately that I go from the apartment to the office and back again.

"And I don't want to complain about the way things are. I know we've come a long way, but as a single woman, the social scene can be limited. It's much easier for a man."

"Tell me about it," said Mary.

"More so in a small town. When I studied in Montreal, it was a different world, throw in a company of artists and free spirits, and there are things I would not tell my mother!"

"You also went to a Paris art school, didn't you?"

"Yes, in 1926, enrolled at the Académie Colarossi. They accepted female students AND allowed us to draw from nude male models, imagine that! It will be a while before I can hang any of those sketches in my house. It could seriously impact my status as a Sunday School teacher if it was widely known in town." They both chuckled at the idea.

Chapter 11

Peter practically ran into the office with a folder in his hand, ready to reveal what he had learned on his Merrickville outing.

"You know what surprises me all the time, Aunt Liz? It's how much people are willing to talk about other people, more so in a small town.

"I said I was a student researching and interested in the book Josephine Smith had written about Scottish history in that area."

"Good idea; what did you find out?" asked Elizabeth.

"Susan came with me, and we had to take her sister as a chaperone. So, I told Susan only the minimum about the case, and she thought my acting skills were excellent. So much more exciting than just going out with an accountant," laughed Peter.

"But that's not what you want to know, right?"

Peter continued, "Josephine Smith was born in Merrickville, and her father is Canadian, but her mother is American. You already know that she was involved with the historical society. She had a broader involvement in Brockville, Gananoque, and Ottawa.

"Also, many dealings with upper officials, both in Canada and the States, even fundraising to buy an island in American waters to create an international park. None of these projects seems to have been completed.

"Financially, it's hard to see where she might have gotten her money. The father was not well-off, and she didn't have steady employment, but nothing was said about anything out of sorts with the fundraising."

"She has two sisters, a Mrs Hoss in Omaha and a Mrs Jones in Philadelphia. A few library patrons also said she was a forceful woman and did not take no for an answer, not without a fight anyway. They also said they had not seen her in town for a while. She moves around quite a bit."

"Are you sure they said a Mrs Hoss in Omaha, not Philadelphia?" asked Elizabeth.

Peter looked at his notes and said,

"No, that's what I have written down Omaha, Nebraska."

"That is strange because Mr Drew said she had sent the book by mistake, along with some clothes, to her sister Mrs Hoss in Philadelphia," said Elizabeth.

"One would almost think it's a game if she sends a box to a Mrs Hoss in Philly. Aside from Smith, no one trying to retrieve it would make that connection.

"Along the same line, if the box is uncollected and the shipping company tries to .contact the recipient, she doesn't live there, so she would not reply to any communication. Brilliant!"

"But to what end?" asked Peter.

"It keeps her in play, no one can bypass her to get at the book," said Elizabeth.

"If the Fenian Brotherhood or Drew were trying to get around the middlemen, in this case, the middle woman, they wouldn't know where the book is. So, they need her; it guarantees her safety."

"I'm going to contact Drew and see if he has any news from her," said Elizabeth as she picked up the handset.

"Mr Drew, this is Elizabeth Grant from the Lefebvre PI office. I thought I would reach out and see if you have heard anything from Josephine Smith. But unfortunately, there is nothing new at my end, I'm afraid."

"Mrs Grant, I was going to contact you. I won't need your services much further. Miss Smith heard that I was looking for her and was quite displeased by the search flyers I put out there.

"She said that she was in Cornwall. The book had not come in as promised, but she was going to Philadelphia on Thursday to retrieve it. She promised to return it very soon."

Elizabeth thought that very unlikely, but she said, "I'm glad for you that all will be resolved, Mr Drew. I will be forwarding our final invoice in the post this week. But, again, it was a pleasure working with you."

Her next call was to Edward Rushton to bring him up to date.

"I'm going to Philadelphia on Thursday," explained Elizabeth.

"We will book a return trip to ensure you have a seat. Then, if need be, you can always re-schedule the departure date. Just be careful, Elizabeth."

She put the handset back in its cradle and turned to Peter.

"So, you know what comes next, right?" Are you good for a few days of cat-sitting?"

"Of course, he knows me well now. Aunt Liz, can I ask you something?"

"Sure, anything, you know that," replied Elizabeth.

"It's about Susan."

"She's not in trouble, is she?"

He blushed and exclaimed, "Oh, Aunt Liz…of course not. It's something else, you know, when we went to Merrickville together, we had a lot of time to talk in the car, and she confided in me."

"Well, I noticed before that, but Susan never has any money. Not that I expect her to pay for anything if I'm taking her out, but I can tell sometimes she's embarrassed."

"She told me that her mother never has any money either. Her father gives her mother what she needs for groceries, and she has to return the change. The same for Susan's train for school; she only has the exact amount."

"Is the family having hard times?" asked Elizabeth.

"You know, many people have very little money these days."

"No, I don't think they are doing too badly. Her father is a supervisor at the paper mill, so it's a steady income and not a large family. Susan told me her mother makes most of their clothes. Susan always looks beautiful, but she can't get things like other girls at school."

"Susan is thinking about getting a job now that school is ending, but her father told her she would have to give him everything she earns. It's right to contribute to room and board once you work, but giving everything seems unfair.

"I never really thought much about it before," he continued.

"I remember my father giving my mother his pay envelope every Friday. He would take a few dollars for himself, and my mother would make sure everything was taken care of. We weren't spoiled, but we had everything we needed. I thought it was how most married people handled it."

"Unfortunately, Peter, it's not the case," said Elizabeth. "And there isn't much a woman can do about it."

"I'm sorry about that," said Peter.

"Susan's birthday is coming up, and I'm not sure what to give her now that I understand what is going on at home. What do you think would be a nice gift?"

"With winter coming, perhaps a nice pair of leather gloves. A woman always likes nice, good quality gloves. They last a long time, and she would always think about you when she wears them."

"Excellent idea," said Peter.

"You can try at Mayfair's Ladies Shop, down on Pitt Street; you can mention my name, they know me there," said Elizabeth.

"Maybe you can come with me? I'm not sure I'm ready for ladieswear talk yet," laughed Peter.

Chapter 12

Elizabeth dressed comfortably for the long trip, wearing a black skirt with a knit top with a matching cardigan in blue, the mandatory hat and gloves, and a light raincoat for the cooler September days. She packed as lightly as possible and stopped by the bank to get some American money for the anticipated expenses.

She picked up her ticket from Cornwall's north-end railroad station a little after 6 pm. The departure was set for 6:45 pm, and the train would arrive in New York at 7:30 am the following day. From there, she would transfer from New York to Philadelphia.

Only a few passengers were on the platform that evening. Most were men, and it was easy to spot Josephine Smith based on the description she had compiled and the feathered hat that seemed to be her trademark. Elizabeth kept some distance between her and Smith but noted which car she entered. The railway agent looked at Elizabeth's ticket and directed her to another coach further down.

Because this was an overnight trip, she was in a Pullman sleeping car with twelve sections, each with double-facing sofa seats. Those converted to a lower birth, and what looked like an upper storage area was, in fact, an upper birth that would drop down when needed. As she was travelling alone, she had an entire section to herself, and she must remember to thank Edward's secretary who had booked it. She settled in with a magazine but closed it after the two-page spread on the Marcel wave hairstyle. She noticed an older lady sitting alone across from her, so she asked if she could sit with her for a while.

"Absolutely, my dear, please take a seat; I'm Mrs Eastman; call me Ruby. It will be lovely to have company."

"I'm Elizabeth; it's nice to meet you."

Mrs Eastman was fiddling with some papers in her handbag, finally pulling out what looked like a passport and studying the photo.

"Those passport photos can be dreadful, don't you find?" asked Elizabeth as an opener.

"Oh, no, I love my photo, it's the picture of an old biddy, but it's MY picture."

Elizabeth didn't quite understand, hoping she didn't offend the older woman.

"You see, I didn't have a passport of my own before my husband died. My husband had one, and I had my photo alongside him, but it was under his name. I was a small note at the bottom that said, "and wife", no name."

"Can you imagine that! Five kids, I ran the house and kept the books for his business, but there I was, just a footnote! Not much you could do about that in those days, really not much you could say "no" to if you wanted peace in the house."

"That was meant to discourage women from travelling alone, wasn't it?" asked Elizabeth.

"Travelling alone, you say…I had five kids at home and a husband who couldn't boil water for his own tea. So where was I supposed to go alone? Holidays abroad? I don't think I had a day off in 48 years!"

"So, when my husband died, the first I did was get my own passport. I may not use it much, but I'll be darn if I die a footnote."

Elizabeth laughed and said, "You have a wonderful sense of humour, Ruby."

"Sometimes that's all you have to get you through one day to the next," she said.

"My husband wasn't a bad man, he wasn't hard on the kids, but he was twenty years older than me when I married him. My father thought it was a good match. It makes sense that I'd outlive him; he gave the house to our oldest boy, but I got a little money. So, I went to visit my sister in Cornwall, and I'm returning to my daughter in New York."

"But that's enough about me. Tell me about you, my dear Elizabeth."

They chatted for another hour before deciding to retire for the night. Elizabeth's section had an upper and lower birth with a privacy curtain. Fortunately, she had the section to herself and did not plan on doing any of the acrobatics needed to climb on the upper birth. Instead, she pulled the cushion from the facing seats and converted them to a lower birth. She settled for the night and fell asleep quickly, the train movement more soothing than she had imagined.

The following day she was up early and dealt with the challenges of getting dressed and ready in such a confined space. She smiled as the images of a travelling couple assigned an upper birth ran through her mind.

She had time for a quick bite from the café car before arriving at the New York station. Disembarking at the New York station was hectic, with people and luggage going every which way. The terminal was a large building, and trains from every corner of the country merged into this connecting hub. So, there she was, glad to stretch her legs for a few minutes, picking up postcards on her way back. Her next train was scheduled to leave at 10 am and arrive in Philadelphia at 1 pm.

An announcement was made on the platform that the train to Philadelphia was delayed due to a breakdown, and the new expected departure would be noon with an arrival of 3 pm. In Elizabeth's view, this was not a bad thing, because it would give her more time to figure out a plan. But, of course, many of her actions would be determined by Smith's movement on arrival. So, it was a wait-and-see game for now.

She went to the snack bar for a coffee and wrote postcards to a few friends to pass the time, saying how wonderful this vacation was. No doubt they would wonder what prompted this sudden getaway, but right now, sitting alone in New York, she needed the connection the writing provided. The trains took the mail in twice daily, and they would get the postcards before she returned. She wrote a long letter to Peter, knowing he might be the only one to understand what was happening here. She was apprehensive, wondering what she was getting herself into. A middle-aged woman, a housewife who went from steaming envelopes for fraud cases in Cornwall to an international caper well above her pay grade. Ultimately, she was more scared of what her daughters would do to her if they ever found out.

A touch before noon, she found herself on the station platform again. There were more people, and it took her a few minutes to spot Josephine Smith. This time she got in the same car, allowing her to go in first. The layout was different for the shorter trip, with a centre aisle, double-facing seats on one side, and single seats across. Elizabeth sat a few seats away from Smith, discreetly observing her.

Josephine Smith was a good-looking woman who would have been called stunning in her younger days. She had a theatrical air about her, as though every door was a stage entrance, an opportunity to find the best light for her profile. Elizabeth had noticed this in her physical posturing but also in her interactions with others. She had observed Josephine talking with other passengers and railway employees, both men and women, and her demeanour was different each time. It seemed that she quickly assessed people and was either cajoling, praising, or even overbearing, whatever the upper hand called for. She parleyed those skills into getting a window seat when none were initially assigned to her or even readily available.

Elizabeth settled in to read *Life Begins at Forty*, a new book by Pitkin, dubbed a "self-help" book. She was curious, given that she was already fifty, wondering what she could look forward to. After two hours of what the author would no doubt see as personal growth, she followed Smith to the dining car. She knew she should keep a low profile, but she had come across the name of Josephine Smith some thirty years ago, and now there she was. It was too much to resist.

"Excuse me, would you mind if I sat with you? The lunch car is terribly busy," asked Elizabeth.

"Not at all," said Smith as she introduced herself.

"Thank you very much; I'm Elizabeth Grant. I noticed you also started your trip from Cornwall."

"Yes, I'm on my way to Philadelphia on business," said Smith.

"What a coincidence, so am I," said Elizabeth. "I must attend to some dreadful business with my late husband's business affairs."

The remaining conversation was light, and lunch was quickly over. Elizabeth returned to her seat, not wanting to draw further attention to herself. Instead, she read some more and closed her eyes for a portion of the trip.

When the porter announced their destination, Elizabeth gathered her bag and kept an eye on Smith. She had not planned every detail of this journey, so her mind was racing on what to do next. Finally, Smith hailed a cab and said, "Morris House Hotel, please." Elizabeth followed.

Chapter 13

The Morris House Hotel was in the city centre, a lovely three-storey brick building of Early American architecture built in 1787. Elizabeth did not enter immediately but gave Smith time to check in. If she recognized her, staying at the same hotel coincidences can only be pushed so far. The main entrance was through a private courtyard enclosed by a black wrought iron fence. The front desk was next to a small dining room overlooking the inner garden. The walls had bookshelf inserts with a broad selection of reading material. Unfortunately, Elizabeth would not be able to enjoy the space openly for fear of running into Smith. Elizabeth booked a single room for one night.

"I have a friend who should be arriving soon, or maybe she is here already," Elizabeth asked the front desk agent.

"Miss Josephine Smith, do you know what room she is in?"

"I can't tell you her room number, privacy, you understand," said the clerk, but he did look to the key rack.

"But I can tell you she has checked in; would you like me to ring her?"

"No, that will be fine. I will go and freshen up first," said Elizabeth, noticing that the only key missing in the direction he was looking was for room 315. She was one floor below; that was perfect.

Early the following day, Elizabeth walked up to the third floor and peeked down the hallway. She did not believe Josephine had left for the day yet, so she waited. Finally, the door to 315 opened, and Elizabeth sneaked into the broom closet next to the stairs. With Smith on her way downstairs, she came out of hiding and went down the hall. The maid had started her daily service with the newly vacated room. Elizabeth jumped at the opportunity.

"Excuse me, but there is a lady next to the stairs, she seems to be in some pain or distress. Could you have a look," said Elizabeth feigning a sense of urgency.

"Yes, madam, let me see what I can do," replied the maid.

Once the maid was out of view, Elizabeth entered the room and looked around. She noticed paperwork and letters in the wastebasket. She dumped the content in her bag and stashed the larger pieces under her sweater. Then, she quickly went back to the stairs.

"There is no one there, Madam," said the maid.

"Oh, well, perhaps she managed to get downstairs. Thank you for your concern."

Elizabeth went down to her room and sorted the papers she had collected. A discarded draft of a letter to the local branch of the United States Express Company here in town, asking for boxes to be shipped back to Cornwall, and an old, crumpled bill of lading addressed to a Mrs John Hoss of Philadelphia. She had no time to lose and would need to find that box with hopefully a rare book inside before Smith went out for the same purpose. She threw on her hat and coat and grabbed her suitcase, again going on instinct as to what to do next. She scribbled on a piece of paper and used a hotel envelope to seal it.

She stopped at the front desk. "Would you give this message to my friend Miss Smith in room 315, please?" asked Elizabeth.

The unsigned note read,

Meet me in the lobby at 10:30 am today.

That would give her enough of a head start before Smith realized no one was coming. She hailed a cab that would take her to the United States Express Company at the Reading Terminal, a short distance away. The complex was massive, and it took Elizabeth a few minutes to finally find the storage company's office.

"Yes, Mam, how may I help you?" asked the employee behind the desk.

"I'm here to pick up a box. I have a bill of lading here." Since there was no Mrs Hoss in Philadelphia, Elizabeth thought she could pull this off.

"Oh, that is a very old piece of paper. Do you happen to have any other identification?" he asked.

Elizabeth pulled her best Greta Garbo expression, near to tears, and explained,

"I don't have anything with me, and these are items that belonged to my dear departed husband. Can you help me?"

"I see here that there are two boxes, a smaller one and a quite larger box; there is also an amount due before I can release anything," said the clerk awkwardly. "The amount is $8.51; these boxes have been here for a while. I see that we tried to contact you but to no avail."

Elizabeth had to take a gamble, there was no way she could manage a large box, and she hoped the book would be in the smaller of the two.

"I can only pay part of the amount, and I don't have much on me. Can I take only one box? The smaller one? I could pay $7.51, leave the other box in good faith, and pay the remainder when I return for it?"

"Yes, I expect we could make such an arrangement," he said as he returned to retrieve the box.

Elizabeth took the small box and went to the nearest public washroom. She quickly opened the box, and lo and behold, a small worse-for-wear book was under a pile of woman's clothing. Elizabeth shoved the book into her handbag, closed the box, and returned to the storage company.

"Excuse me. I was thinking, after all, that I would prefer to come back and take both boxes. So, I will give you back this one and will be back later today for both. How's that?" asked Elizabeth.

The clerk looked slightly annoyed, and Elizabeth did not wait to discuss this further. Instead, she walked out of the United States Express Company, jumped into a waiting cab, and said, "30ᵗʰ Street train station, please."

From the station, she called the hotel; she had paid everything in advance and notified them she was checking out. Elizabeth was looking for the earliest train possible leaving Philadelphia to go to New York. She found it preferable to wait for the evening train to Cornwall in the relative safety of the larger New York station. Her main fear was that Josephine Smith would figure out her deception and catch up to her. She figured she had a start of about two hours. She expected Smith to be quick on the uptake, given her history.

Elizabeth felt safe that she had not been followed to New York yet and arrived in the late afternoon with a booking on the overnight train to Cornwall, leaving at 7:20 pm and arriving home at 8:25 am the following day. Again, she had her section and settled in early. She still had the book in her bag and had not dared to take it out. In the closed surrounding, she now felt very curious about the object of so much desire, fraud, and trickery.

She took the book out of her bag very gently, as though she feared it would fall to dust from being handled. It was a small book with just 138 leaves, bound in leather over those wooden boards Hope had mentioned. There were some decorations impressed in the leather on the front and spine. The date "1548" was impressed at the bottom of the front panel. On the fly leaf inside, words were scribbled imprecisely as though the writing was rushed. Drew had said the writing named Father Conificus, but she was unsure about that. The paper seemed sturdier than what she had imagined for a book this old. The written words she could not understand or identify. As it stood there in her hands, it was a rather unremarkable book if not for its age. She wrapped it up again and carefully placed it in her bag. She tossed and turned all night, anxious to see what tomorrow would bring.

Chapter 14

Back in Cornwall, after another long train trip, Elizabeth was exhausted. It was a combination of physical fatigue and excessive mental stress. She had never been so glad to see her small apartment and Dusty lying on her bed. She proceeded to call Edward.

"I have the book," she said. "It must have taken ten years off my life!" She explained what had happened, and Edward seemed impressed with her resourcefulness. He told her someone would be down to get the book in the coming days.

"I need to see the game plan now; as I said, we want the transaction with the Fenians to take place here, so we need to work that out. Thanks again for doing this."

"I am taking a few days to rest, putting my feet up, and listening to the radio. Then, I have a dinner to look forward to. I don't think I'm quite cut out for the spy game as I thought I was," laughed Elizabeth.

Elizabeth was looking forward to the Kinsmen Club Fundraising Dinner that night. Her "let's see where it goes" motto made her feel good about accepting Harry Warner's invitation. It had been a while since her last dinner date, so she paid particular attention to her outfit. Luckily for her, her size had not fluctuated much since leaving Ottawa, so she could fit into a dinner dress that was not new to her but would be for the dinner companions, at least.

She realized she had left her wallet in the office and went up to get it when she heard the door open behind her. As she turned around, she was surprised and scared to see Josephine Smith standing in the doorway.

"Well, hello there, Mrs Grant," said Josephine. "Or, more appropriately, my train companion Cornwall to Philadelphia! Where is my book?"

"How did you find me?" asked Elizabeth.

"I made my way to the storage company only to find out someone else had already looked at the box. It was easy enough with the description from the clerk at the storage company to connect the dots," replied Josephine.

"You told me you were from Cornwall, a few questions in town, and here we are. A word to the wise, if you're going to play the detective, don't use your real name."

Josephine pulled a small pistol out of her bag and said, "Where is my book?"

"Well, on its way to Ottawa by now, heading for the Department of Justice, actually," said Elizabeth.

"You bitch! Do you know what my life will be worth if I don't give it to the Fenians?" screamed Josephine.

"And you can't return it to Drew, and the Mounties know all about your scheming; you duped everyone," said Elizabeth.

"It was going to be an easy job, stealing a stolen book, once I realized the value of it, but that idiot Drew just wouldn't let go," said Josephine.

"You know why I did it, of course; it's the money. Selling the book would put me in danger but at least the money from the Irish I could take. At this point in my life, living from pillar to post, the spinster sister, moving from relative to relative, the money would mean my independence, you understand."

"Yes, but when the Fenians convert the book to cash, it could hurt others, a great many more people, I'm afraid," said Elizabeth.

Her mind was racing, trying to figure out what she could do or say next. Oddly enough, all she could think about, of all things, what how small the gun was.

"Turn around," Josephine said.

Elizabeth turned towards the window, hoping someone would see her figure from the street and help her. She heard the clicking sound of the gun but it did not fire. That was her last hope before she felt a sharp pain on the side of her head. Josephine had hit her with the one of the heavy bookends from the desk. Elizabeth`s knees gave way as she fell to the ground.

Josephine knew she had not played this game well. She needed a way out. So, she moved the waste basket under the drapes, and set the content on fire. If Elizabeth had lied and the book was still in this office, at least no one else would get it. Josephine ran out of the office.

🌿

"Harry, stop looking at your watch; it looks like you got stood up," said Bob, Warner's top mechanic."

"We'll see," replied Harry.

He looked around for Peter Darvis, whom he had seen coming in earlier. He was sitting with a group from the business college, and he called him over.

"Hi Peter, did you hear from your aunt Elizabeth?" asked Harry.

"I asked her to the fundraiser, and she said she would meet me here, but she didn't show up yet. Of course, she might have changed her mind about coming, but I didn't think she would without letting me know."

"It wouldn't be like her to stand you up, Mr Warner; she's very good at her word," said Peter.

"I'm wondering if anything is the matter. This case we have been working on is very tense now, maybe…."

"Ok, let's go by the office and see. It won't take long," said Harry.

Harry and Peter walked out of the Cornwallis Hotel and turned south on Pitt Street. Daylight was fading, but Peter noticed a woman coming out of the building and walking fast toward the end of the street and the canal.

"See there, that's not Aunt Liz, but that lady seems in a hurry to get out," said Peter.

They both picked up the pace, and Harry said, "Look, the office window, there is a light, a flicker, like a fire. I'll go up, and you stop that woman."

Harry ran up, two steps at a time, and pushed open the office door, Elizabeth was lying on the ground beside the desk, and the place was filling up with smoke. He ripped the curtain off the rail and used it to smother the fire in the wastebasket. He reached over to Elizabeth, and she started to move, moaning and coughing. He helped her up, and she focused on him, touching the bump on her head.

"Are you all right?" asked Harry.

"Let's get out of here into the fresh air."

"We need to call the police, Harry, and tell them to call Ottawa, the Mounties; they will know what it's all about," said Elizabeth.

Outside she took a deep breath and leaned against the wall. Peter came running.

"I couldn't catch her; she fired at me," he said.

"When she turned around, and I saw the gun, I jumped into a doorway, and she kept going towards the canal. How are you?"

"You cannot imagine how happy I am to see you," said Elizabeth.

"I have a headache, and I need a drink! How did you know something was wrong?"

"You didn't show up for dinner. It was a leap of fate that you wouldn't do that to me, so I got Peter, and we decided to check on you," said Harry.

"I'm glad you did; I'm glad you did."

Some of the canal workers had noticed the commotion, heard the gunshot, and called the police. Elizabeth filled them in on what happened, and they recommended that she get medical attention.

"I'm taking you to the hospital. Can I have your car keys?" asked Harry.

Before they left, she heard officer McDonnell report to his superior that the canal crew had seen someone jump in and were "fishing her out now."

Harry took Elizabeth to the Hotel Dieu hospital on Water Street. He sat with her while she waited to be seen by a doctor. He realized she was now beginning to grasp the danger she had been in, and the silence was heavy.

"I didn't realize when I gave you the fluffy charcoal kitten that you would end up having so much in common," said Harry.

Elizabeth couldn't help but smile. "Yes, and thanks to you, we are both enjoying our second life. I'm sorry you missed your dinner."

"It's all good; there will be other dinners," he hoped.

Chapter 15

Elizabeth was released from the hospital with a clean bill of health, a prescription for headache tablets, and rest. A worried Edward Rushton had left messages at the hospital and tried to contact Peter; he was relieved when he heard back from her.

"I'm glad you're all right," said Edward.

"We brought in Drew and Lawson. Lawson didn't want to be in trouble any more than he already was, so he told us everything he knew. The same for Drew. As for Smith, word came in from some higher-ups to stop the interrogation. The orders came from the British Government, 10 Downing Street no less."

"Strange, do you know why?" asked Elizabeth.

"Rumours are, and you've worked in government, so you know those should generally be believed, that the British want to talk to her, something she might know, a spy in the ranks, maybe. I'm unsure how it relates to the book, but it's out of our hands now."

"I told Smith the book was on its way to you, but of course, you know I still have it," said Elizabeth.

"There is something about it; I would like to get it checked out. Can you meet me at *James Hope & Sons* on Sparks Street, say 2 o'clock?"

"Sure, I'll bring an RCMP officer with me. I'm not taking any chances; see you there."

Elizabeth drove up to Ottawa in good time. She was now sitting at a café overlooking the bookstore, waiting for Edward to show up. She was trying her best to look and, more importantly, feel very casual about this whole process but kept a close eye and both hands on her bag. She jumped up and walked towards them at first sight.

"Hi, Elizabeth; I don't know if you met Inspector Frank Santini. He was at the hospital; he brought Smith back," Edward introduced the officer.

Santini nodded but did not speak. He was tall, thin, and wore glasses over a face that said very little, as though expressions came from an account in which he had no funds. Elizabeth could imagine his second career as a successful poker player.

John Hope immediately saw them, putting on a pair of white cotton gloves before handling the book.

"This is so exciting. You understand that one doesn't get an opportunity like this every day."

He gave the book a thorough inspection and shook his head.

"It is a nice piece but not what your Mr Drew claimed. It is written in middle Scots, but it's not a prayer book. It's not the right style for that. Let me see; we receive notices from libraries and booksellers internationally with a list of stolen or known to be missing books. The aim is to stop the sales of such books. I have something here for the Library of Scotland."

He continued, "*The Complaynt of Scotland* is listed as missing from their collection. The author is anonymous… thought initially to have been printed in Scotland but was recently confirmed as printed in France. The book was part of a war of words between Scotland and England, propaganda, really. It was dedicated to Mary of Guise, not Mary Queen of Scots."

"How much do you think?" asked Elizabeth.

"It would be valuable for the library that owns it, you understand, but for anyone else, around $1,000, if that," replied Peter.

"Then, I don't understand all the drama; why are the Fenians so interested in getting this book back?" asked Edward.

"It was stolen three times! First, brought into the country by a British citizen, and then Drew steals it; Smith does the same and sends it to the States for what we believe is a profitable sale. It seems the Fenians or their sympathizers are ready to kill for this, and there's pressure from the British."

"We're missing something," said Elizabeth.

Hope took another look glancing at the flyleaf. "You see this name here?"

"Yes, Father Conificus," suggested Elizabeth.

"Well, the writing is not original to the book," said Hope as he scrutinized the entry with a magnifying glass.

"It's a common mistake in handwriting; the shape of the letters is not always that clear, especially when the writing is faint. I could see this one as being Father Cornelius."

He showed Elizabeth, "See how the *r* and the *n* come together, and the extension below of the *l* is very short, the first stroke of the *u* is curved, no, I think it says, *Father Cornelius.*"

"So, who in the blazes is Father Cornelius?" asked Santini, who had stayed with his back to the door.

"The Venerable John Cornelius, Roman Catholic Priest from an Irish family," Elizabeth surprised everyone, including herself, with the identification.

They all looked at her, "Catholic upbringing," she said.

"Yes, but his real name was John Connor O'Mahony. But, hey, I sell bibles and religious books!" he smiled.

"Who's our High Commissioner of Trade for Ireland?" asked Edward. "Clarence Mahony!"

"Clarence Orville Mahony," added Santini.

"And Father Cornelius was born in Cornwall, England, and Clarence Mahony was born in Cornwall, Ontario. He moved up from political life to a promotion as High Commissioner!" said Elizabeth.

"That's our man, a Canadian used by both the British and the Irish! Let's go tell tales," said Edward.

They thanked John Hope. Santini took the book and walked out.

"I'll let you know what's next, Elizabeth.

"We would still like to put the Clan out of action in Canada; it's a tangled web," said Edward.

Most unexpectedly, Santini smiled and said, "Give that woman a raise!"

Elizabeth droved back to Cornwall to await news and see what the Department would do with the information they had just uncovered. They were still no closer to getting their hands on Josephine's contacts.

Chapter 16

Elizabeth was not party to all the negotiations between government officials, the police, and Josephine Smith. Still, it was agreed that Smith would set up a meeting to catch the Fenians on the Canadian side.

The book was still in play, and the Fenians were none the wiser about what the police and government knew. Josephine was to offer the book to her contact and arrange a meeting to hand over the book in exchange for her finder's fee. Because of the inability to close the deal in Philadelphia as initially planned, she had lost her leverage in the negotiations and took a substantial loss from the initially promised amount the Clan had offered her, $1,000, not bad considering the average factory worker was getting thirty cents an hour. Of course, she feigned outrage but agreed, as Santini told her.

"There's no way in hell I'm letting Smith do the deal; she can't be trusted," said Santini.

"How about Mrs Grant? Would she be willing to finish the job? What do you say, Rushton? Then, we can set up a transaction in Cornwall."

"It might assure the Fenians that it's not set up, a small town, easy access," said Rushton.

"I wouldn't blame her if she didn't want anything to do with us anymore, though."

Rushton called Elizabeth and told her of their plan and asked if she wanted to help them again.

Without hesitation, Elizabeth agreed. In *for a penny, in for a pound* was the old saying, and she wanted the case closed once and for all.

Once again, Rushton and Santini made their way to Cornwall. A little after 6 pm, Santini unfolded a map of the waterfront on Elizabeth's desk.

"The exchange will happen in the park area of the Stormont Mills, just as you cross the Augustus Street bridge here, onto their property. It's a swing bridge, and we ensured it would stay open for traffic."

Rushton went on, "There are two small buildings on that side, a gatehouse for the bridge operation and a shed. We have already placed policemen in both of those this afternoon. We believe the Fenians will either come in or leave by the water. That choice of location signals that it is set on the open waters."

"Where will I be," asked Peter.

"Nowhere close, Peter; you're a civilian," said Rushton.

"Absolutely not! I'm going. I'm a detective, she's my aunt, and I have already been shot at, so there is no way I won't be there. Besides I know the area even in the dark," insisted Peter.

Picking his battles, Rushton agreed to a compromise, with Peter staying on the street side of the canal side as a passerby. He could signal an intrusion on that side.

"You, Elizabeth, will take a bag containing a replica of the book in case they want to see it before they give you the money. No matter what happens after that, walk away back to Peter. Santini and I will be out of sight behind you."

"Did the contact ever meet Josephine Smith?" she asked.

"Would they recognize her?"

"Around the same age, we can cover the different build with a larger coat, and she said she would be wearing a hat with a feather in it. The light will be dim; you should pass," said Santini.

Elizabeth didn't know whether she should be flattered or insulted to be considered some generic fill-in, but she had met and talked with Josephine, so she could at least mimic her tone.

At 6:20 pm, Santini said, "Places everybody, curtains up in ten minutes, let's get this show started."

It wasn't lost on anyone that Inspector Santini was a theatre lover!

Elizabeth left her office and crossed the street to the shops lining Pitt Street. At that moment, she wondered where she was when they taught, "Sound Judgement 101." She obviously missed that class; otherwise, she would be home now knitting socks and reading Victorian romance novels. But no, she was on her way to a secret meeting with a political rebel.

As she passed the high stone walls that wrapped around the old jail courtyard, she couldn't help but remember Mary's story. The Fenians imprisoned right here who had escaped in 1866, a continuity in the thread of history. At the courthouse, she turned right on Water Street. The bridge spanning the canal was at the foot of Augustus Street. She put her collar up and walked across, noticing a man approaching her from the water's edge.

As she put her foot on the bridge, a man reached for her from the left.

"Give me the bag, lady," he motioned to grab it as she hugged it tighter. She knew this was not right because out of the corner of her eye, she could see a man on the other side of the bridge running towards them.

"Let go of her, you British *fecker*," he yelled in an Irish brogue.

All was coming to a head with guns drawn. Elizabeth dropped the bag and ran towards Peter as the guard house door opened, and the Mounties tried to make sense of it all. A smaller group ran towards the water's edge to grab those trying to get in the waiting boats.

Elizabeth and Peter stood in the middle of the street while Santini and Edward ran to the scene. The Mounties were rounding up those left behind and clearing the scene.

"It's all over," said Edward.

"We lost a man, a shot in the crossfire, they did as well, but we have the rest."

"Showdown like in the western movies, Mrs Grant," Santini exclaimed.

"We didn't know anyone else was coming to this party, and I apologize for that. But given that everyone is spying on everyone else, agents and double agents, I'm not surprised. This plan leaked like a sieve."

Elizabeth promised to call Edward in a day or two, and Peter took her home.

"Coffee, Aunt Liz?" Elizabeth declined but opted for a Scotch on ice, small glass, large shot.

"Aunt Liz, promise me this is over. My nerves are shot and I'm not even twenty years old yet!"

"I hear you. It's not doing anything good for my grey hair, either. I think we've seen the last of this case."

Elizabeth told Peter to take a few days off and sent him home.

Chapter 17

Secret Intelligence Service Section 6, 54 Broadway, London England

Josephine Smith had been escorted, courtesy of the British government, from Ottawa right to the door of Colonel Alan Stanfrey, a senior official with the British Secret Service, the international section known as MI6. She had to smile; it was a long way from Merrickville, Ontario, to downtown London, a long road and a lifetime away.

She knew Alan, Sir Alan then, a dashing young diplomat eager to make his mark in the foreign service. And made his mark he had, on her certainly, when they first met in 1903. She fell for it, the aristocrat, the fancy dresser, the charming accent, but she landed hard when he moved on.

Back then, she travelled freely between Canada and the States to see her family. A cousin had told her about the Fenians. She became part of their circle and learned of their meetings and plans. She had reported on them, becoming an informant with the Canadian Department of Justice. She met Alan in Ottawa, and he took an interest in her, or rather in the potential of her abilities to find out information. Through him, she was assigned more work. Her good looks and friendly approach were a sure way to get information. She was active well after the first world war and then sparingly until the Drew affair and the stolen book.

"Col. Stanfrey will see you now," said a young lieutenant.

And there he was, heavier, older, with a grin she wouldn't trust for all the money in the world, sitting behind a large oak desk, worse for wear, both him and the desk.

"Hello, my dear; I must say it is nice to see you," he said, smiling.

"It seems I had to bail you out once again. Too many questions from your government might not be good."

"Not great for me, but certainly terrible for you," she said.

"Oh, come on, play nice now. You and I go way back," he protested.

"Yes, we do go way back, and I was right there between your wife and your mistress. It was a bit crowded if I remember."

"In another life, we might have had a future together," he tried that smile again!

"Tell me, what movie are you in right now? she asked.

"There is no "other" life, only this one, at a time when both of us are re-arranging rocking chairs on the porch, not getting extra people in our beds."

"But I did care for you, you know," he said.

"Perhaps, in your way, but you soon pawned me off to the Irish and the Americans. In those days, you would have rented your own mother to further your career. King and Country, I know. But do you know where old spies go when it's all said and done?"

"Are you looking for a retirement home?" he asked.

"Why should I help you any further? Your service to us is over."

"Let's see, for thirty years, I have been drinking champagne with all shapes and sizes of diplomats and agents. I have been listening, but who knows if I reported everything or what else I found out along the way?"

"I love to write; it's a passion of mine, keeping diaries, making lists. And as I was less busy in the trade in recent years, I had time to write my memoirs."

Colonel Sir Alan Stanfrey turned an uncomfortable shade of white and said, "What do you want?"

"A retirement plan, a little income, a safe place, perhaps somewhere warm, small town. I could spend my last years writing mystery novels."

"My memoirs are safe now, but any newspaper could get a copy if things don't go my way."

"The book is with a friend?" he asked.

"No, with a respected foe, which should worry you till your last breath."

"Ok, I will arrange a small income, a relocation, pick a new name," he surrendered.

"You drive a hard bargain."

"You taught me well, my love."

🍃

Elizabeth loved fall, the crisp air, the colours and the sun's reflection on the calm waters of the St. Lawrence. The recent events had given her a greater appreciation for time and leisure. Her daily walk had taken her down by the harbour, her favourite spot. She could never tire of watching the ships and the tugs go about their business. She walked across Central Park and found a courier waiting for her when she returned to the office.

"Are you Mrs Elizabeth Grant?" he asked.

"I need a signature, please."

Elizabeth signed and received a thick envelope in exchange. She went to her office and was curious to see what this was. She wasn't aware of anyone sending her work files.

There was a card attached to the cover page. It read:

> *Keep this safe for me; I trust you to know if and when it might be needed.*
>
> *Josephine Smith*

Elizabeth looked at the envelope, it was sent from Saint-Lunaire, France, and the sender was J. S. Simmons. She put the manuscript back in the envelope and dropped it in her small office safe. How strange, but then this case had always been about a book...

Ginette Guy Mayer

Conclusion

"Mother, anything you want to tell me. Like, who's Josephine Smith, and what have you been up to? Do I have to read about you in a copy I'm editing for *The Journal?*

"And there's more that our reporter tells me can't go in the article… And who is Harry Warner, really, mother?" fired Muriel over the phone.

Elizabeth wondered when this unruly child had become the parent.

She remembered that *The Ottawa Journal* had a reporter in Cornwall and that coverage was daily.

"Oops," thought Elizabeth.

"Hi Muriel, why don't you come down this weekend, and we can go over your high school years?" said Elizabeth.

"Well, you are not in high school mother, and I didn't do mine in Philadelphia, so what's going on?" said Muriel.

"Wait till I tell Margie, you're in big trouble."

"So, it's set then; you're coming this weekend? I have to leave now; I'm meeting a friend."

"You're not going to tell me anything over the phone, so yes...count on me bright and early Saturday; see you then. I love you, Mother."

Elizabeth added a bottle of wine to her shopping list.

Her second call was from Edward, asking how she was and apologizing for putting her in this life-and-death situation again.

"You're a real trouper; enormously proud of you, you know. The Fenians were not saying much at first, but once we told them we had figured out the message in the book, they had no choice.

"We're looking into the British involvement in all of this. There'll be a domino effect, I'm sure. I asked that they look back on the death of the British tourist who brought the book in at Drew's gate. It seems he was poisoned, made to look like a heart attack. He knew what was coming but wouldn't know where the book would land. So, he wrote down the name of that priest, knowing the Fenians would figure it out if they got their hands on it.

" The High Commissioner of Trade for Ireland, Mr Mahony, has been called back and may soon be enjoying a discreet retirement.

"Well, seeing you again was anything but boring, I must admit," said Elizabeth.

"Time for all of us to take a break. You know you should bring Julie down and come for a plain old sightseeing visit one of these days."

"Yes, absolutely, we have been talking about getting away. But, you know, on a personal note, one good thing came out of all this work. I was away so much and working late that Julie realized she missed me; it's been good for us."

"I'm so glad, Edward, you deserve the best," said Elizabeth.

"You let me know if you come down."

🍃

Elizabeth and Mary were having tea at Fullerton's Tea Room, going over recent events, and Elizabeth pushed *The Standard-Freeholder* newspaper onto the table.

"See page 3, left column, *Ottawa Returns Rare Book to Scotland National Library*; it's an interesting read," said Elizabeth.

"It was returned to their Special Collections. There is also something about some commotion on the waterfront again, on page 8."

"Page 8, really?" said Mary.

"I'm sure the Mounties made recommendations to the local police on that one," explained Elizabeth.

"How did you figure it all out?" wondered Mary.

"With the help of Edward Rushton from the Department of Justice, some things I had worked on in the past, I just made connections, leaps, and bounds," said Elizabeth.

"In the end, a Catholic education saved the day. Josephine Smith was a very smart woman and used much creativity in moving the book around. It was hard to track; only she knew. Still a lot of unanswered questions about her, though."

"What a peculiar case, one that put your life at risk, though; I'm so glad you are all right. But that being said, I have a new idea you could help with."

Mary explained her idea for an arts association in town. Elizabeth was excited about the project; it was something new to look forward to.

"I'm thinking of perhaps two art shows and two concerts per season," said Mary.

"I know many artists who would love to share their work, maybe a few short lectures, and we could get schoolchildren involved. It would give them their first exposure and make a lasting impression."

As Elizabeth nodded, Harry Warner walked in and stopped by their table.

"Good day, Miss Randolph, Mrs Grant, nice to see you; I see you have recovered well...again.

"I'm picking up a few treats for the guys' lunch break. Bob's wife is not well, and I'm afraid he is lost and can't put a decent lunch together for himself."

"That's very nice of you, Mr Warner," said Mary.

"Miss Randolph, I was wondering if one of your volunteers might be able to drop in on her and see how she is doing?" asked Harry.

"Certainly, mother knows her from the church group, and we will go and see her; perhaps we can help."

"Thank you, that is very kind of you. Hopefully, it's nothing serious."

"Mr Warner, we are discussing an idea I have for art shows and music concerts, an art association here in Cornwall," said Mary.

"Would that be something that would interest you, say, a string quartet? Would you get tickets, hypothetically speaking, of course?"

"Well, that would be nice. Some of the things available in larger cities, right here at home," Harry replied.

"And, of course, an evening like that would be nice to share with a friend. I could even buy two tickets if you put in a good word on my behalf and get a friend, say someone working in a P.I. office, to accompany me to such a concert, hypothetically speaking, of course.

"I'm sure we can work on that, Mr Warner," smiled Mary.

"Yes, we can work on that," echoed Elizabeth as he walked to the counter to pick up his order.

The two friends walked out, one going to a meeting, the other back to her office. Elizabeth had to consider options to get extra help. Eventually, she would have to replace Peter. She contemplated her desk and the pile of filing she needed to do, calls to deal with, and new cases to manage. Then, finally, life was back to normal.

A knock at the door brought her back to reality, and a man walked in and removed his hat. He was in his late thirties, in a well-tailored suit. He smiled as though he knew something amusing and said,

"Good day Mrs Grant. I'm Frank Lefebvre, a private investigator."

Elizabeth nearly choked on the sip of water she just took.

"I am a private investigator in Montreal, and I was recently made aware of your role in certain cases and excellent abilities," he continued.

"I'm thinking of expanding and thought we could discuss, say, a merger, Lefebvre & Grant, Private Investigators? It looks like the writing is on the wall."

Elizabeth laughed and said, "I might be thinking more of Grant & Lefebvre, but please take a seat and let us see where it goes."

Photos

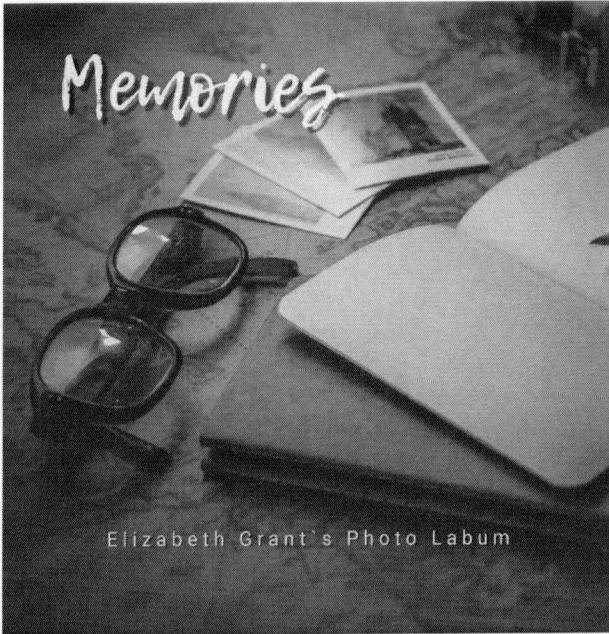

Elizabeth Grant's Photo Labum

When we shared this case file with you, we realized that we showed you things and places that might not be familiar to you.

Elizabeth thought she would share some of her personal photos with you, with the aim of providing extra background to this case.

We hope you enjoy them,

Ginette Guy Mayer on behalf of

Elizabeth Grant

1-Fire on Pitt Street in 1933

2-Pitt Street at the corner of Second Street looking
north. The left side shows the area before the 1933
fire.

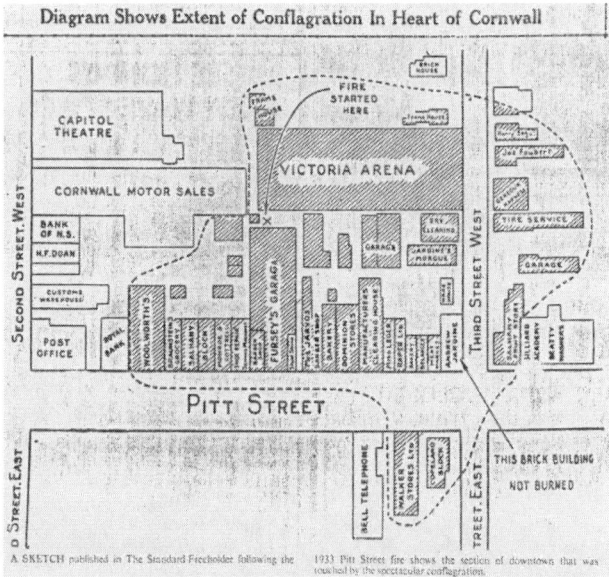

3-Diagram as it appeared in the Standard-Freeholder of August of 1933. The buildings in dark shade were lost to the fire.

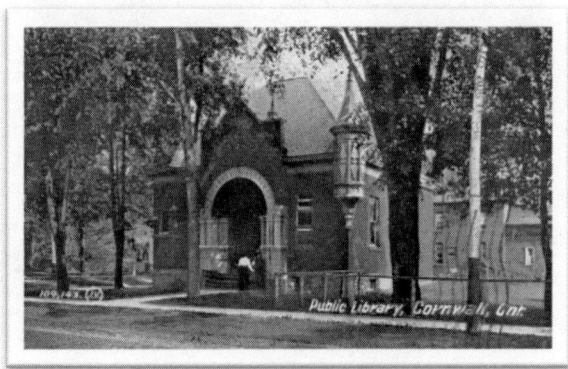

4-Carnegie Library, southwest corner of Sydney and Second Streets.

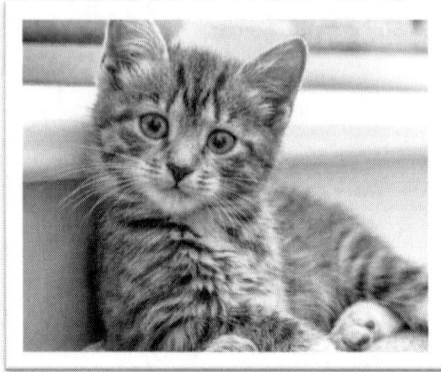

5-Elizabeth's kitten Dusty, a present from Harry Warner.

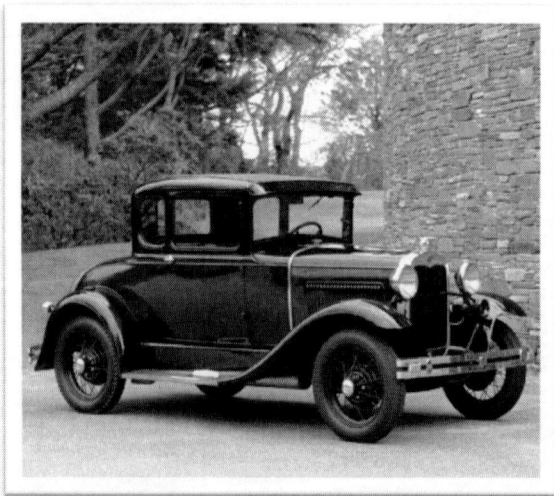

6-Her 1930 Ford Coupe Model A bought used from Warner's Garage.

7-Cornwall's north end train station.

8-The Royal York Café on Pitt Street where Elizabeth took Edward Rushton for lunch.

9-A Pullman sleeping car, showing the upper and lower birth, the same layout as the Cornwall to New York leg of the trip.

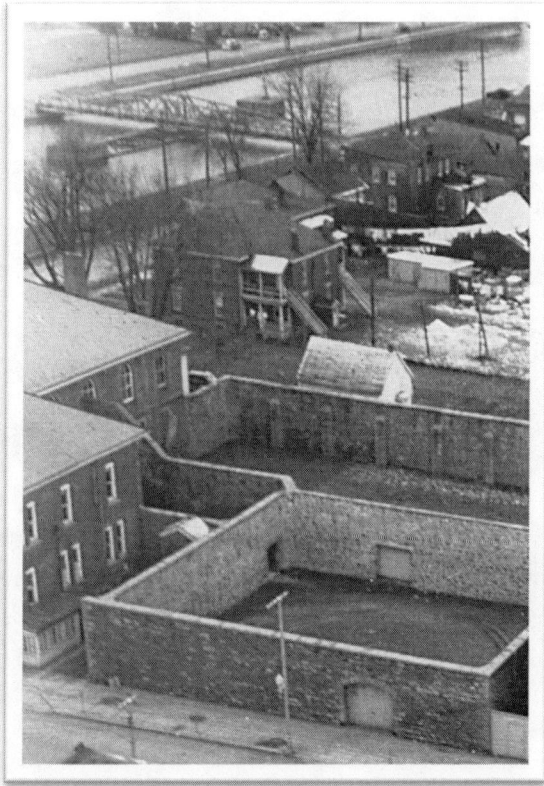

10-This is the bottom of Pitt Street, the building in the foreground is the County Courthouse and Jail. The stone wall and the jail yard that Elizabeth walked past on her way to the Augustus Street swing bridge shown at the upper part of the photo.

GENERAL VIEW OF CORNWALL CANAL, CORNWALL, ONT., CANADA.

11-Postcard showing the Augustus Street swing bridge on the left, canal along Water Street. To the right is the park on the Stormont Mill side where the meeting with the Fenians and Elizabeth took place.

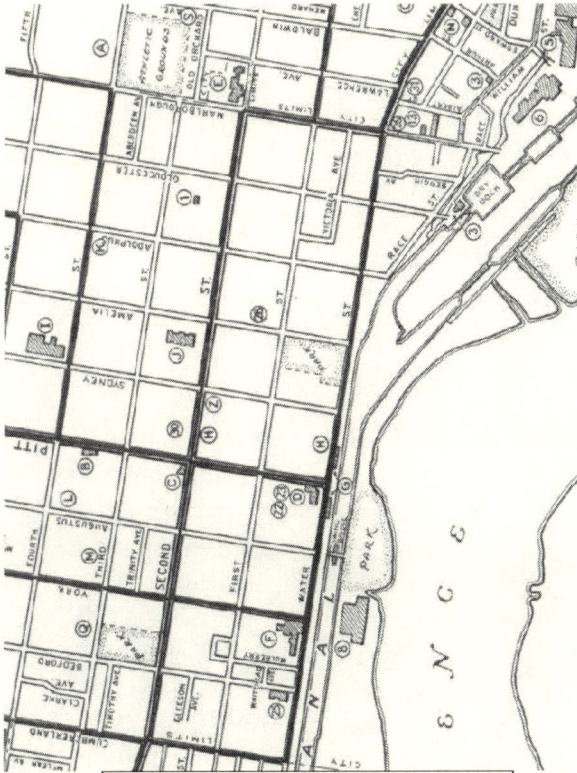

Map showing some of the streets and areas mentioned in the case file. Shows the canal in relation to the river and the park where Elizabeth met the Fenians at the Stormont Mill

8- Stormont Mills
D- Counties Courthouse & Jail
F- Hotel Dieu Hospital

Photo Credits

1- Fire on Pitt Street – Cornwall Community Museum/SD&G Historical Society, 1933

2- Pitt Street before the fire – Cornwall Postcards, c. 1930

3- Diagram showing the extent of the fire damage –Standard Freeholder, August 8, 1933

4- Carnegie Library – Toronto Public Library, Public Domain, c. 1910

5- Dusty the cat – Public domain web photo

6- 1930 Ford Coupe Model A – Public Domain web photo

7- Cornwall Train Station – Canadian National Railways/Library and Archives Canada, Restrictions: nil – Copyright: expired c. 1926

8- Royal York Café – Cornwall Postcards, c. 1930

9- Pullman Sleeping Car – Flickr from No22, unaltered from the Chicago History Museum, c. 1930
https://www.flickr.com/photos/no22a/25130 59082/

10- SD&G Counties Courthouse and Jail – Canal view from the Stormont Mill, postcard, Cornwall Community Museum/SD&G Historical Society, c. 1930

11- Postcard of waterfront – Cornwall Community Museum/SD&G Historical Society, c. 1930

12- Map of downtown Cornwall – Industrial Committee City of Cornwall, 1950

Manufactured by Amazon.ca
Acheson, AB

11435942R00076